The
New Woman

OTHER WORKS BY JON HASSLER

FICTION

Staggerford
Simon's Night
The Love Hunter
A Green Journey
Grand Opening
North of Hope
Dear James
Rookery Blues
The Dean's List
Keepsakes and Other Stories
Rufus at the Door and Other Stories
The Staggerford Flood
The Staggerford Murders

FOR YOUNG ADULTS

Four Miles to Pinecone
Jemmy

NONFICTION

My Staggerford Journal
Good People . . . from an Author's Life

The
New Woman

❧

Jon Hassler

VIKING

VIKING
Published by the Penguin Group
Penguin Group (USA) Inc., 375 Hudson Street, New York, New York 10014, U.S.A.
Penguin Group (Canada), 90 Eglinton Avenue East, Suite 700,
Toronto, Ontario, Canada M4P 2Y3 (a division of Pearson Penguin Canada Inc.)
Penguin Books Ltd, 80 Strand, London WC2R 0RL, England
Penguin Ireland, 25 St. Stephen's Green, Dublin 2, Ireland
(a division of Penguin Books Ltd)
Penguin Books Australia Ltd, 250 Camberwell Road, Camberwell,
Victoria 3124, Australia (a division of Pearson Australia Group Pty Ltd)
Penguin Books India Pvt Ltd, 11 Community Centre, Panchsheel Park,
New Delhi – 110 017, India
Penguin Group (NZ), Cnr Airborne and Rosedale Roads, Albany,
Auckland 1310, New Zealand (a division of Pearson New Zealand Ltd)
Penguin Books (South Africa) (Pty) Ltd, 24 Sturdee Avenue,
Rosebank, Johannesburg 2196, South Africa

Penguin Books Ltd, Registered Offices:
80 Strand, London WC2R 0RL, England

First published in 2005 by Viking Penguin,
a member of Penguin Group (USA) Inc.

1   2   3   4   5   6   7   8   9   10

Publisher's Note
This is a work of fiction. Names, characters, places, and incidents either are the product of the
author's imagination or are used fictitiously, and any resemblance to actual persons, living or
dead, business establishments, events, or locales is entirely coincidental.

LIBRARY OF CONGRESS CATALOGING IN PUBLICATION DATA

Hassler, Jon.
The new woman : a Staggerford novel / Jon Hassler.
p.   cm.
ISBN 0-670-03455-X
1. Staggerford (Minn. : Imaginary place)—Fiction.   2. Older people—Housing—Fiction.
3. City and town life—Fiction.   4. Older women—Fiction.   5. Minnesota—Fiction.   I. Title.
PS3558.A726N49 2005
813'.54—dc22
2005042262

Printed in the United States of America
Set in Simoncini Garamond
Designed by Leonard Telesca

For Clare Ferraro

The
New Woman

1

Agatha McGee had been a resident of the Sunset Senior Apartments only three days when she realized that she'd lost the diamond brooch her parents had given her when she'd graduated from Staggerford High School in 1927. Having spent the morning looking for it until she was too exhausted to stir herself for lunch in the dining room downstairs, she sat in her rocking chair by the window and absently watched the traffic pass below her on Main Street. Sunset Senior was a long, two-story building abutting the business district, and Agatha was thought by her friends to have the best room of all, front and center and only a few steps from the elevator. From this vantage point the town looked strange to her. It was a much busier place than she'd thought. Having spent her eighty-seven years looking out the windows of her house on River Street, she had carried around the image of Staggerford as a bucolic, serene little hamlet, and she was under the false impression that she was still acquainted with all its citizens, as she had been in her teaching days. But now, watching cars pull in and out of the lot in front of the Kmart across the street, she realized that there were hundreds of people living in this town whom she didn't know.

But more important than the realization that she was a has-been was the matter of the diamond brooch. She brought to mind that evening seventy-one years ago when she had been called onstage four times—to receive her one-hundred-dollar scholarship as class valedictorian; the letter S she'd earned for being captain of the Girls' Athletic Association; the new Ingersol wristwatch given as the Citizenship Award that year; and finally, with her twenty-seven classmates, her diploma. It had been such a family affair that Agatha had to smile at the memory. Her father had delivered the commencement oration and her mother had been in charge of the punch table. Before leaving for the ceremony, her father, a demonstrative little man for that day and age, had given her a hug and a kiss when he presented her with the brooch, and so had her mother after pinning it on her dress. Agatha was so proud of it that she unpinned it and wore it outside, on her graduation gown, throughout the evening.

She was drawn out of this pleasant memory by the sound of the elevator opening across the hall. Lillian Kite came knocking on her door. "Agatha, are you in there?"

"Yes, I'm here."

"Are you all right?"

"Of course. I'm fine. Why wouldn't I be?"

"You weren't down for lunch."

Oh, dear, this move was certainly a mistake. Agatha had feared that living here would compromise her independence. She should have paid attention to her hunches instead of her friends and stayed put in her house on River Street. At home she'd never in her life had to answer for missing a meal. Except, of course, when her doting parents were still living, but that was different. Her parents had been sincerely concerned about her welfare, while many of these old biddies at Sunset Senior were merely curious snoops.

"Open up, Agatha. Let me look at you."

Agatha sighed and lifted herself out of her chair. She couldn't very well turn away Lillian, her friend since girlhood. For the last several years, since Agatha had become more or less homebound, Lillian had dropped in at least five afternoons a week to help her with household chores—washing sheets, dusting, doing the dishes in the sink. Although Agatha had never thought of her as a soul mate—Lillian's tastes ran to the *National Enquirer* and soap operas—she was grateful for the woman's friendship, and in particular for her mulish strength and stamina.

"You look a little peaked," said Lillian, peering for a moment at Agatha and then going to the window to look down on Main Street. "I'd say you ought to take it easy for a day or so before you get back to unpacking."

"Oh, I'm finished unpacking." Agatha pointed to a pasteboard box filled with crumpled paper next to her rocker. "I've been looking for my diamond brooch. I remember seeing it, but I don't know what I did with it."

"You know, I think that's Mabel Becker across the street. What's she doing downtown? I thought she was in the hospital with her gallstones."

"I've looked high and low for it, Lillian. It was a gift to me when we graduated from high school. Do you remember what a lovely spring evening it was? Apple blossoms—"

She was interrupted by Addie Greeno, who, seeing Agatha's door open, came in complaining about the eating habits of old John Beezer. "He eats like an animal," she said in her very high and irritating voice. "Just puts his head down and shovels it in."

Agatha pulled her door shut behind Addie, making sure it was locked.

Lillian said, "Addie, do you know who I just saw going into Kmart? Mabel Becker, but I was told she was in the hospital with gallstones."

"I say the very least you can expect at mealtimes, if not tasty food and interesting company, is table manners. How can you sit across from John Beezer and watch him eat, Lillian? It makes me sick just thinking about it."

"I'm going to call the hospital and ask them what's up."

As Lillian dialed the phone on the table beside the rocking

chair, Agatha answered a knock on her door, calling, "Who
is it?"

"Edna Brink," said a deep voice. "What are you girls doing
in there?"

Agatha opened the door and Big Edna Brink came barging
in. "Are you girls getting up a bridge game? Because if you are,
I'll make a fourth."

Addie Greeno repeated her complaint to Big Edna. "I've got
half a mind to go right down and tell Joe or Little Edna about it.
Have them put up a sign about table manners."

Big Edna, at once the largest and nosiest resident of the Sunset Senior Apartments, took in the room, studying Agatha's furniture and the pictures on the walls. Then seeing the box filled
with crumpled paper, she said, "Land sakes, been here since Saturday and you aren't unpacked yet, Agatha?"

"Oh yes, I'm unpacked all right. I was looking for a diamond
brooch I seem to have misplaced."

"How much did it cost?" asked Big Edna.

"I have no idea what my father paid for it in 1927, but it was
appraised a few years back for quite a lot of money."

"How much?"

Actually it was three thousand dollars, a sum Agatha couldn't
bring herself to utter. "Quite a lot," she said.

Putting down the telephone, Lillian said, "Weren't we told
that this was the week Mabel Becker was going to have her
gallstones seen to? Well, Mercy Hospital says she was never
admitted."

"When I think of how he chews with his mouth open!" Addie Greeno shuddered and added, "That does it. I'm going
downstairs and talk to Joe and Little Edna this minute."

"Don't talk to Joe," Big Edna advised. "Little Edna's the
manager."

"I know who the manager is, but her husband, being a man,
will get things done."

"Don't kid yourself, Addie. He's got Parkinson's."

Agatha got everyone's attention by asking, "Have any of you lost anything to robbers here at the Apartments?"

"Robbers!" squeaked Addie Greeno, and Big Edna laughed her low rumbling laugh.

"Just checking," said Agatha. "Wondering if my brooch has been stolen."

Lillian said, "No, Agatha, no robbers," and she added that she was going across the street and ask Mabel Becker about her gallstones.

"I'll go with you," said Big Edna, following her out of the room and telling her to put on a jacket; it was cold outside.

"I'm going down and speak to Joe and Little Edna," said Addie, following them both out.

Agatha shut her door, again making sure it was locked, and settled into her rocking chair to ponder the incivility of Big Edna Brink's inquiring about the cost of the brooch. It was enough to make her entertain the possibility of moving back into her own house. Although she'd signed a quitclaim deed putting it in the hands of her grandnephew Frederick Lopat, the property was still hers in spirit. Frederick would welcome her back. He'd said as much last Saturday when he'd helped her move into Sunset Senior. Saturday being his day off from the Willoughby Post Office, Frederick had borrowed a truck from a friend and loaded it with the precious few items she'd need to furnish these three rooms, including this padded rocking chair in which her mother had nursed her when she was a baby. But as Frederick was helping her out to the truck, she'd stalled in the doorway. It was as though she were paralyzed. She couldn't move, and she might be standing there yet if Frederick hadn't said, "Come on now, Agatha, you can always move back if it doesn't suit you." To which she had responded by bringing her considerable willpower to bear on her body and forcing her legs to carry her out the door.

2

The ice storm had blown in several days earlier, the week after Thanksgiving, snapping branches off trees and laying them across power lines until practically everybody in town was without electricity. Frederick brought in a big pile of wood to keep the fire stoked in the fireplace, and it wasn't until Agatha left the living room to go to bed that she realized how terribly cold the house had become.

She slept fitfully through the night, pressed down by several blankets, two quilts and an extra bedspread. She woke in the morning to find that Frederick, having brought in a new supply of wood, had gone off to his job at the post office, eight miles away. From her front window she saw that the ice and sleet had been followed by a blizzard that made streets impassable and would probably delay the repairmen from the power company. Frederick called at noon to say that he couldn't finish his mail route and to ask how Agatha was getting along.

"No trouble so far," she said from her rocking chair, which she'd moved over in front of the fire, "but please hurry home. I've already used up more than half the wood you brought in."

"I'll be there inside of an hour," he'd told her. But snow kept piling up through the afternoon, and Frederick phoned again to say he was sorry but the highway was blocked and he wouldn't make it home that night. A momentary wave of panic overtook

Agatha until he assured her that there was more split wood on the back porch.

But there wasn't much, certainly not enough for another full day of burning. In order to conserve the wood, she crawled under her blankets and quilts in the early evening. Luckily her water heater still held warm water, so she had her hot-water bottle to keep her feet warm in bed. During the night she awakened several times with a fit of coughing and she knew that she had caught a cold. She woke up early in the morning and found that her bedside lamp was lit and her furnace fan was blowing heat into her bedroom. She said a prayer of thanks for electricity, and she petitioned God never to let this happen again.

But her troubles weren't over. She heard water running somewhere and she got out of bed to investigate. Her kitchen floor was flooding from a burst pipe under the sink. She went halfway down the cellar to turn off the water valve and saw water spraying from two broken pipes down there. She phoned Mayor Mulholland, formerly the city engineer and city clerk, and got his wife, Beverly, on the phone. Beverly promised to send her husband over right away.

Both William Mulholland and Beverly showed up within five minutes and found Agatha choking on phlegm. Beverly whacked her on the back, then comforted her while William explained that the water had frozen and burst the pipes and now it was thawing out and escaping. He set to work replacing the pipes.

Frederick showed up then, having followed a snowplow from Willoughby, and was alarmed to see Agatha wracked with coughing. Speaking from his own experience with pneumonia, he said it sounded serious, and Agatha permitted herself to be bundled up and driven to the clinic.

Beverly accompanied her into the examination room. Dr. Hammond detected trouble through his stethoscope and recommended that Agatha go into the Care Center for a few days.

Picturing the Care Center, which was attached to Mercy Hospital and where she had visited certain old friends on their way to the cemetery, she said, "I may look ancient to you, Doctor, but I'm only eighty-seven and it will be some time before I become a basket case, thank you very much."

"But she can't continue to live alone in that house," pleaded Beverly to the doctor. "Frederick is gone five days a week and she could choke to death. Besides, she doesn't eat right."

"Piffle," said Agatha, sweeping haughtily out of the examination room. "It will be quite some time before I'm ready for the Care Center."

When they returned to the house on River Street, the pipes had been fixed and William Mulholland was already gone. Beverly and Frederick deposited Agatha in her rocking chair, which they moved from in front of the fireplace to the window overlooking the street and the river beyond; then Frederick asked Beverly if she wanted a ride home. He was eager to get back to his mail route.

Beverly said yes, her unstable son Owen was staying at her house for a few days and needed constant supervision. "But Miss McGee can't stay alone," she said.

"Of course I can stay alone," said Agatha. "I've lived alone all my life. Besides, Lillian will be along soon."

Beverly said, "I'll call Linda Schwartzman."

Which Agatha permitted her to do. She was fond of Linda Schwartzman, her neighbor and friend, and she didn't see nearly enough of her because she was kept so busy as Staggerford's only mortician. Linda happened to be at home. She said she would come to Agatha's house immediately.

It took her nearly half an hour, during which Agatha sat alone at her front window watching the snow from the day before being picked up and blown about by a cold north wind. For the first time in her life she felt afraid of her house, whose electricity and pipes had betrayed her. If the blizzard had lasted one

more day, she herself would have been frozen as hard as the water in her pipes. Surely there would be more ice storms and bliz-
zards, and what could she do but die? When Linda finally
arrived, looking vigorous in her jeans, long coat and scarf, and
pink cheeked from her walk down the street against the wind,
she asked Agatha how she was feeling, and her reply was, "I've
been brooding over a sense of my mortality."

This sort of surprising candor was what Linda liked best
about her old neighbor, but she couldn't get Agatha to elabo-
rate, and soon Lillian came in with the news that the central
second-floor apartment overlooking Main Street, in Lillian's
opinion by far the best apartment at Sunset Senior, had just
opened up because Thelma Thorkelson had dropped dead at
lunch not twenty minutes earlier, and this was Agatha's chance
to snap it up for herself. Lillian, to no avail, had been urging
Agatha for years to join her at Sunset Senior, and now, when
Agatha said, "I'll come and look it over," she was shocked
speechless.

"You mean . . . ?" Lillian paused in unknotting the char-
treuse scarf wrapped tightly around her neck. "You mean . . . ?"

"I mean I'll take a look at it. I'll have Frederick drive me over
tomorrow when he gets home from work, and if I like it, I'll
want to talk to somebody about finances." She explained then,
to both of her visitors, about her night and day spent alone,
about the lack of power and the burst pipes. She didn't go into
her cold. Her coughing told them all they needed to know about
the state of her health.

"We didn't have but a minute's outage at the home," Lillian
bragged. "We have a generator that makes its own electricity
when the power's off."

"I'll drive you over there now, if you want to go," Linda
Schwartzman offered.

"No, thanks," said Agatha, waving the thought out of exis-
tence. "I've already been out once today. One trip outdoors is

the limit at my stage of life." This prompted an explanation of where she'd been and an inventory, at Lillian's request, of the people she knew in the clinic waiting room.

Agatha had already visited the government-subsidized Sunset Senior Apartments several times, as she had the Care Center, but she had not yet met the new manager, a certain Mrs. Edna Rinkwitz, who told her that the room would cost one fourth of her monthly income, and it was Agatha's because her name was first on the waiting list, but if she didn't take it today, it would go to the next name in line.

"You're mistaken," said Agatha, "I never entered my name on a list."

"Oh, yes," said Mrs. Rinkwitz, showing her a list of six or eight names with her own at the top.

She thought Lillian must have put it there. "Well, I'm afraid I'll have to pass up the opportunity," she said, glancing at the Rinkwitz's apartment, beyond the office where they were sitting. It seemed to be packed with knickknacks. "The rent is beyond my means."

"But surely one fourth of your income is reasonable," said Edna.

"Well, you see, I have a hundred thousand dollars in the bank at seven percent—that's seven thousand—and a small retirement benefit from teaching of about four hundred. So I'd be paying—let's see, twenty-five percent of seven thousand four hundred—why, I'd be paying you nearly two thousand dollars a month when I have a perfectly good house to live in rent free for the rest of my life."

"I'm afraid you're wrong, Agatha," said Mrs. Rinkwitz, and she saw Agatha stiffen. Being new in town, she didn't understand that Miss McGee was never wrong and never addressed, except by close friends, by her first name. But today Agatha *was* wrong. Mrs. Rinkwitz explained that the seven percent interest on her bank balance was an annual amount, and that it brought in, per month, only—here she picked up a pencil and divided seven thousand by twelve and came up with a humiliating pittance that caused Agatha to get up and leave the office without another word.

"Call your banker and ask him," Mrs. Rinkwitz called after her and added, "I could be wrong."

Agatha did so as soon as she got home. Her banker, Alfred Gossitch, said, yes, her interest per month amounted to a little over $583, not $7,000.

Agatha, never a whiz at numbers, asked him how that was possible, since her principal amount had been growing steadily over the years. She recalled that the savings account had stood at under forty thousand dollars when she'd inherited it from her father in the late fifties.

"It grows because you spend so little," said Mr. Gossitch, and he added, evidently looking at her checking account on a computer screen, "You wrote several checks to a travel agent in the eighties and early nineties—I seem to recall that you went to Ireland—but other than that you've never spent your entire interest for the month."

She then asked him to add her $400 teachers' retirement income to the $583 and multiply the sum by twenty-five percent. The result was approximately $246.

She thanked Mr. Gossitch and hung up without telling him that that was the amount she'd have to pay Sunset Senior each month for her room and board. Although nowhere near the $2,000 she'd assumed at first, it seemed like an outrageous amount. She hadn't written checks as big as $246 since Garvey Travel arranged her flights to Ireland.

The next day, Thursday, after Lillian left, Agatha coughed so violently that she lost her balance and fell down in the kitchen, hitting her head on the door frame and becoming unconscious for several minutes. When she came to, she called to Frederick to help her to her feet before she realized he had gone to work and wouldn't be home for another hour. It was while lying there, frightened and chilled, that she decided that $246 was little enough to pay for having neighbors in the next apartment who would come to her aid.

3

Trying to overcome her worry about the brooch, Agatha went down to supper in the dining room, arriving early so that she could get her favorite spot at the farthest table from the door, avoiding the nasty draft let into the room when the front door was opened. Agatha had been wary of drafts all her life, and especially since her recent respiratory difficulties.

She watched the crude retired farmer John Beezer arrive with the fastidious Thaddeus Druppers, a former grocer. These two had been more or less forced into an unlikely friendship by virtue of their being the only men living at Sunset Senior. Seeing Agatha, Thaddeus made a beeline for her table, as she hoped he would do, for they had been friends for a lifetime, and John Beezer followed. They sat down opposite her and Thaddeus said, "This is Agatha McGee, John; she taught school in town here for almost half a century."

"I know it, the new woman," said John, glancing up from his broken fingernails but not looking Agatha in the eye. He asked Thaddeus, "Is she going to the Blue Sky?"

"What's the Blue Sky?" asked Agatha.

"It's a casino," Thaddeus told her.

"A gambling casino?" she said. "Certainly not."

"She ought to come along," John said, still speaking to Thaddeus. "Everything's free."

"How are you, Thaddeus?" Agatha asked, changing the

subject. Thaddeus, his face as wrinkled as an old leather glove, was a year older than Agatha. They'd known each other in elementary school and had since served together on various boards and committees of St. Isidore's Church.

"Fine, Agatha. And you?"

"Worn out from searching through my apartment all day. I've lost a valuable piece of jewelry, and I've decided it was stolen."

Thaddeus's wrinkles formed themselves into a look of concern. "Stolen. Oh, I don't think so, Agatha. I've been here more than two years and I've never heard of anything stolen."

"Well, that surprises me, the way everybody leaves their doors unlocked."

"Oh yes, most of them never think of locking up. In fact, I don't know where my key is at the moment."

"I keep my door locked at all times." Agatha fingered the key hanging from a string around her neck. "Whether I'm there or not."

"Yes, I know. Edna Brink told me." Thaddeus chuckled. "You'll get over it."

"Free lunch, free gambling," said John Beezer. "The bus over and back is free."

Next to enter the room were Lillian Kite and Big Edna Brink. Their friendship didn't surprise Agatha. Each was curious and meddling in her own way. Besides reading the *National Enquirer* and watching television, Lillian was forever looking out windows to see whom she recognized on the street, while Big Edna patrolled the hallways, listening in at doors to see what the residents were up to. With Lillian covering the world at large and Big Edna concentrating on Sunset Senior, they gathered a great deal of fascinating hearsay.

"Did you find your jewelry?" asked Big Edna, taking the place on Agatha's right. The folding chair creaked under her weight.

Agatha shook her head.

John Beezer asked Thaddeus, "Are they going to the Blue Sky?"

"I don't know, John—why don't you ask them?"

John Beezer, apparently shy in addressing women, shrugged and studied his fingernails.

Lillian opened a very large plastic bag and took out something bright colored and voluminous she was knitting and set to work with her needles.

Addie Greeno entered with three other women from her end of the second floor. Addie was one of the few other residents Agatha was acquainted with. For years and years she'd been Father Finn's housekeeper, until the priest was put out to pasture by Bishop Baker and replaced by the current pastor, Father Healy. Addie used to lord it over her friends because Father Finn made her welcome to sit down with himself and his visiting clergy to eat the food she'd cooked for them. As if her friends cared, thought Agatha. If their table talk was anything like their sermons, clergymen must have been the most boring of dinner companions. Agatha had to admit, however, that Addie had been Staggerford's prime source of interesting churchly gossip. But those days were long gone. Now she'd apparently become Sunset Senior's prime authority on the eating habits of her housemates.

At exactly five o'clock, many other elderly women flocked in until the dining room was nearly full. Everyone grew uneasy waiting for the manager and her husband to take their places behind the steam table, where covered pans brought in by a caterer were kept warm. The food was prepared each day by student chefs at the vocational school, and Agatha, who lacked kitchen skills, thought every meal was delicious. An opinion not shared by everyone.

"It'll be ribs and kraut tonight because it's Tuesday," said Big Edna. "I tell you I get plenty sick of ribs and kraut. Then it'll be chicken tomorrow noon and BLTs at night. I get so sick of chicken and BLTs on Wednesdays . . ."

Agatha's attention was drawn to Thaddeus, who'd turned around to look at the doorway and now turned back to tell the women at his table that the servers were late probably because Joe Rinkwitz, the manager's husband, had fallen down in the lobby.

"When?" said Big Edna. "Do you mean on Tuesday?" She turned to Agatha. "Joe fell down coming in the front door on Tuesday afternoon. He'd been out watering the lawn and he fell down on the tile floor and Lillian and I saw him do it, didn't we, Lillian?"

Knitting placidly, Lillian nodded.

Thaddeus said, "No, I mean ten minutes ago. He fell down coming out of his apartment. I happened to be nearby and he gave me a sheepish smile and said, 'Dr. Parkinson tripped me.' "

"Who tripped him?" asked John Beezer.

"Nobody. When he falls down, that's what he says—Dr. Parkinson tripped him."

"Why does he say that?"

"Because it's Parkinson's disease that makes him fall down."

Agatha explained, "It was a certain Dr. Parkinson, an Englishman, who first diagnosed the disease two hundred years ago." This caused John Beezer to look her skeptically in the eye, so she added, "I read it in a book."

There was a round of applause when Little Edna Rinkwitz turned up with Joe, who walked behind her with a cane. The first three tables swarmed, in turn, for their helpings of ribs and sauerkraut and lettuce salad; then Agatha's table went up to the steam table, John Beezer in the lead and Thaddeus bringing up the rear. Big Edna, taking her large helping of ribs from Joe Rinkwitz, asked him, "Did you hurt yourself when you fell down today?"

"No, no, nothing serious, just a bruised knee. Thanks for asking."

These were the first words Agatha had heard Joe utter. He had a soft voice and, it seemed, a soft disposition. He was a good-looking, dark-haired man, perhaps in his middle sixties, though his stoop-shouldered posture (like the pope's, thought Agatha) made him look older. His wife, Little Edna, dishing up the salad, was a small dynamo of energy. She had helped Frederick carry in Agatha's boxes on Saturday and had come by once each morning since to check on Agatha's health and see how she was adjusting to her new home. You never saw her down here that she was not mopping the entryway or vacuuming the lobby or guiding her husband around by the hand.

"We hope your brooch turns up soon," she said to Agatha. "Joe and I are praying to St. Anthony."

Surprised at how fast Big Edna had spread the news, Agatha thanked her. Carrying her food back to her place, she wondered why this couple did such a Catholic thing as pray to the patron saint of lost valuables when she'd never seen them in church. She asked Lillian whether the Rinkwitzes were Catholic.

"Probably, with a name like that," said Lillian. "I mean it sounds Polish Catholic to me."

"But I've never seen them at St. Isidore's."

"Oh, they probably don't go to church."

Agatha winced as though slapped. She'd known others during her long life who had fallen away, but each new case caused her pain. The closer she herself came to the next life, the more of a mystery it was to her that anyone would risk eternal damnation by avoiding the holy sacrifice of the Mass. Church attendance had fallen precipitously among teenagers, she knew that, but the Rinkwitzes were old enough to know better.

Lillian interrupted this train of thought with, "Agatha, did I tell you Mabel Becker never did go in for gallstones?

"No, you didn't."

"It was her sister Marge who had her gallstones taken out and she's sick to this day from the surgery. I guess the anesthetic didn't agree with her. Sick as a dog, Mabel says."

"Who are these Becker women, Lillian? I've never heard of them."

"Sure you have. They were the Sims girls. Mabel married Art Becker and Marge married Tom Becker."

"A bus ride clear to Blue Sky would cost ten bucks, but this one's free ever' Wednesday," said John Beezer to his plate of food, which he was devouring with amazing speed. His hands were greasy from picking up the ribs and a string of sauerkraut was hanging down his chin.

Big Edna said she thought today's fall made three hundred times Joe Rinkwitz had fallen down during the last four years.

Thaddeus said that Little Edna Rinkwitz would have given him another key to his room if he'd asked for it, but he hadn't asked yet.

Agatha, deciding to make John Beezer's acquaintance because he seemed the likeliest jewel thief in the room, touched the back of his weathered hand and said, "Do you come from around here, Mr. Beezer?"

"How?" he said, looking up, startled, his eyebrows raised, his eyes very round, very blue.

"I asked where you came from."

"Room 120."

"No, I mean where did you use to live. You see, I've lived all my life here in town and I don't remember seeing you before."

"Bartlett," he said, referring to a town seven or eight miles to the east. He looked away.

"I see. And did you farm?"

He stood up from the table. "Had a hunnert and forty acres south of Bartlett," he told her, and he turned and walked out of the room, wiping his hands on his jeans.

"He's evidently skipping dessert," said Agatha.

Thaddeus went after him, but returned alone. He explained to Agatha. "He doesn't like to talk about himself. I've known him for the better part of a year and this is the first I've heard him say he comes from over by Bartlett. He said I could have his dessert but I told him they'd save it for him. It's apple pie. It's not good to skip any part of a meal."

"Where did you hear that nonsense?" asked Big Edna Brink.

"Oh, I suppose I read it somewhere. *Time* or *Newsweek* or one of those."

"That's a bunch of bull. The less you eat, the better off you are," Big Edna insisted.

"No, it's best if you eat everything up. There's dietitians that put these meals together who understand what the human body needs."

"The human body sure doesn't need apple pie," said Big Edna.

When Little Edna Rinkwitz came around with a tray of pie, Big Edna asked for John Beezer's slice as well as her own, and she gobbled up both of them in the time it took Agatha to finish her one piece.

4

Agatha went up to her apartment after supper, then thought better of it and went down again to the Rinkwitz's apartment and knocked on the door. She was welcomed in by Joe, who said, "Ah, the new woman."

"I'm sorry to bother you," she said. "I wanted to speak to your wife."

"She's still cleaning up in the dining room, but she'll be here in a minute. Please sit down." Turning to lead her over to a pair of chairs in front of a large TV screen, he seemed to trip but caught himself, bracing his shoulder against the wall. "Sorry," he said. "My balance isn't what it should be."

Analytically looking him up and down, she asked, "Are you dizzy?"

"No, no dizziness. It's just that my muscles don't always support me when I turn around."

"I see." They continued to make their way over to the chairs. Agatha was fascinated by all the things hanging on the walls and crowded on shelves. "My, what a lot of—" she began.

"Junk," he finished for her. "It's all crafty stuff. You see, my wife runs the craft workshop every Saturday and the residents are forever giving her presents." He shrugged helplessly, looking about the room. "This is the latest," he said, plugging in an extension cord attached to a pyramid of baby-food jars in the shape of a Christmas tree. Suddenly it was lit by a tiny bulb in each jar.

"Well, isn't that clever," said Agatha.

"Yes, isn't it," Joe said, with irony showing in his eyes. "Addie Greeno brought it in this week. I tell my wife she's going to have to declare a moratorium on this stuff, or it will squeeze us out and we'll have to move into a different apartment."

Agatha sat down on the edge of one of the chairs while Joe fell into the other. "I'll tell you why I stopped by," she said. "I've lost a precious piece of jewelry and I suspect a robber took it."

Joe was silent, waiting for her to go on.

"So, I've been looking over your residents, trying to pick out the thief."

"Yes? And what have you found?"

"Nobody yet. That's why I was hoping that you and your wife might help me out."

"We had a thief here once; his name was Gerald Hughes. He died many years ago. He was senile, poor man—took things he couldn't possibly use. When we cleaned out his apartment, we found a dozen salt and pepper shakers, for example."

"It's somebody who has a key, because I keep my door locked at all times."

Little Edna came breezing into the room, removing her apron and greeting Agatha with a broad smile and a pat on the shoulder. She said, "I tell you, Addie Greeno will drive me insane one of these days. She won't let me go another day without putting a sign up in the dining room about people's eating habits. She's offended by the way John Beezer chews with his mouth open."

Joe told his wife about the new woman's suspicions, which she dismissed with a laugh.

Agatha, offended, stood up and said, "Of course you think I'm suffering from Alzheimer's disease, but I assure you that although I will turn eighty-eight next fall, I am in my right mind when I say I suspect that I have been robbed."

She angrily made for the door, a move she regretted when Joe hurried to see her out and fell down, his cane skittering ahead of him across the carpet. "Damn it," he sighed at her feet, causing her to back away from him. "This happens every time I hurry."

Little Edna came to help him up, telling Agatha that she'd warned him a hundred times not to hurry. "Every time he walks fast he freezes and falls down."

"Just starting out," Joe explained. "Once I get going I'm fine." Getting to his feet with surprising agility, and taking his cane from Agatha, he added, "Thank you, Miss McGee. This is my three hundred and second fall in the last three years."

"Goodness, you keep a tally, do you?"

"No, no need of that. It happens often enough so that I can easily remember the number of the last one."

"And how many bones have you broken?"

"None, miraculously. But I could show you some bruises."

"Spare me," said Agatha, taking her leave.

Crossing the lobby, she picked up an old issue of *Newsweek* from the lamp table between the two chairs that stood facing the outside doorway. She carried it up on the elevator to her apartment, where she discovered that the lead article had to do with national defense and was dated July 5, 1977. *A twenty-year-old newsmagazine is ancient history,* she thought as she sat down in her rocker and noticed a few flakes of snow blowing past her window. Paging absently through the spread on national defense—bombs, rockets, aircraft carriers—she was amazed at how her interests had changed in the last couple of years. Time was when she'd have been fascinated by this subject, perhaps even written her congressman and senators about it. *Dear Mr. Wellstone, Just a note to make sure you understand the folly of spending millions of our hard-got money on another aircraft carrier.* Now she couldn't seem to spare any attention for affairs outside her immediate surroundings. She was ashamed to think that she'd had nothing on her mind all day but her lost brooch.

Her eye was caught by mention of the MX missile, which was ready to fire and carried on a train that never stopped. That way the enemy would never know where to fire the first strike to knock it out. *How novel,* thought Agatha, *and how preposterous.* She didn't read further to discover that this train traveled only a few miles on a circular track in a western desert. She imagined the MX missile carried round the country, across the South, up the East Coast and then west through the upper tier of states, including Minnesota. She pictured it chugging through Staggerford some night, the missile no doubt concealed in a boxcar with a false roof so that no one, except the crew of the train, knew what the deadly cargo was.

Later, retiring to bed, she had a strange dream in which her brooch was carried around the country on a train. Later she woke briefly and thought, *I must tell Lillian about this; she's always interested in dreams.*

5

The shoebox was Lillian's idea. She produced it from her closet the next morning as soon as Agatha had come down the hall to her apartment and told her about her dream. They would put their valuables in the shoebox and move it from room to room, said Lillian, so that the thief would never know where to find it.

It was a dumb idea, thought Agatha, but Lillian's enthusiasm was such that she couldn't thwart her. "Of course, to make this work, we'll have to have more people involved than just the two of us," said Lillian.

"But we must choose carefully," said Agatha. "They must be trustworthy."

"Big Edna's trustworthy," said Lillian.

Agatha, who didn't like Big Edna Brink, said, "But *is* she?"

"Sure. She's a good old scout."

While Lillian picked up her phone and dialed Big Edna's apartment, Agatha looked around Lillian's room. It was nearly as crowded with ornaments as the Rinkwitzes'. Agatha recalled Lillian telling her that she'd been the Champion Crafter three years running, which meant simply that she'd produced more trinkets than anyone else at Sunset Senior. On the walls were crocheted designs covering spoons, bottle caps and countless other small objects. Hanging on strings tacked to the ceiling were a dozen tiny bells made from Lutheran communion cups.

And Agatha saw that today Lillian wore her newest earrings, which she'd made out of wallpaper and glue. She could picture Lillian working away in the craft room as earnestly and obsessively as she knitted; and she supposed it was good for her old friend to have diversified her interests.

Replacing the receiver, Lillian said, "She'll be right over," and almost immediately Big Edna burst into the apartment, saying breathlessly, "Hi-de-ho, everybody, here I am. What's all this about?" She wore a striped muumuu, and Agatha thought she looked even larger than yesterday. Seeing that the two armchairs were occupied, she pulled up a straight chair from the kitchen area close to them so as not to mishear what she was about to be told.

As Lillian explained her plan, Big Edna leaned into her with her left ear, in which her hearing was somewhat better than in her right. Then she clapped and exclaimed, "An MX Shoebox, what a fun idea!"

Lillian was already dumping the contents of her purse into the shoebox on her lap.

"No, Lillian," said Agatha. "This will be only for valuables."

Lillian was undeterred. "All of this is valuable," she said, picking an earring, a nickel, half a roll of Tums out of the box to prove it.

Agatha, uncomfortable sitting in this tight little circle and unhappy at having to accept Big Edna into the scheme, stood up and went to Lillian's window, which looked out across the alley at a series of Dumpsters standing at the backs of stores. What a dismal prospect. No wonder Lillian loved the view of Main Street from Agatha's side of the building.

"I know exactly what I'm going to put in," said Big Edna with a girlish giggle. "At first just my opal bracelet, and then later, when it proves to work, I'll put in my opal necklace and my sack of rare coins."

"What do you mean, 'when it proves to work'?" asked Agatha.

"I mean if it doesn't get lost or thrown out by mistake. If somebody doesn't open it up and take something out and keep it."

"The box will be sealed tight," said Lillian. "Taped shut. And, for pity's sake, who would lose it or throw it away?"

"The forgetful among us," said Big Edna. "Don't forget this is an old folks residence and a lot of our friends are getting senile. We'll have to choose mighty carefully who gets to be in on it. And nobody gets to have it for more than twenty-four hours."

Lillian said, "Well, I thought a couple of days . . ."

"No, no. One day apiece. I'll go around and move it every morning. Now we'd better make a list." Big Edna drew a ballpoint pen out of a pocket, clicked it open and said, "Lillian, a piece of paper."

Lillian, who'd started knitting, pointed with one of her long needles to a pad of paper under her telephone.

Watching her write *MX Shoebox* on the pad, Agatha resented the way Big Edna Brink had taken over Lillian's project, but at the same time she felt that Big Edna's officiousness and enthusiasm proved her to be as trustworthy as Lillian said she was.

"Put down Addie Greeno," said Lillian.

Big Edna wrote *Addie,* then paused. "I wonder," she said. "Addie might be over the hill. Yesterday at lunch she couldn't remember the name of the family that lived next door to the parish house for twenty years."

"What family was that?" asked Lillian.

"Oh, you know. They had all those cats." She turned to Agatha. "You must remember. The man worked on the railroad."

"No, I don't recall." She remembered the cats but not the name. "Don't single out Addie for a poor memory. None of us can remember the name either."

"But none of us lived next door to them," snapped Big Edna.

Then she softened. "Well, I suppose we can give her a try," she said, writing down Addie's last name. "The more the merrier."

"And Agatha," said Lillian. "And Harriet Hillyard."

"And Thaddeus Druppers," said Agatha.

"And John Beezer," said Lillian.

Having written down the first four names, Big Edna balked at the fifth. "John Beezer's too dumb to understand. Besides, Addie can't stand him."

"Well, with you and me we have six," said Lillian. "That ought to do for starters."

Big Edna agreed. She added Lillian's name to the list, and then, with a flourish of curlicues, her own. She said they would visit Addie's apartment after lunch, as well as Harriet's and Thaddeus's, and collect their valuables. "I'll volunteer to take it the first night," she said.

"No," said Agatha. "We'd better stick to the order of your list. Otherwise we'll forget who has it when."

"I'll make a new list." She was about to tear this one in half when Agatha stopped her.

"No, this is the list we've memorized. A second list would only confuse things. Addie will take the box tonight. Is that all right with you, Lillian?"

"Of course."

Agatha then went back to her apartment and tried to decide what she would put in the shoebox, all the while going over the list in her mind. Addie Greeno, herself, Harriet Hillyard, Thaddeus Druppers, Lillian, and Big Edna Brink.

Who was Harriet Hillyard?

6

At lunch—a chicken drumstick with fried potatoes—when Lillian brought up the subject of the shoebox, intending to tell Thaddeus about it, Big Edna Brink forcefully shushed her. "Never mind, Lillian, he knows all about it." She nodded in the direction of John Beezer and added, "Just remember, loose lips sink ships," quoting a poster she recalled from World War II.

Leaving half her dessert unfinished—tapioca and a dry, crumbly cookie—Agatha followed the little group along the first-floor hallway to Thaddeus's apartment. While Big Edna dug the shoebox out of Lillian's knitting bag and handed it to Thaddeus, Agatha looked over the man's underfurnished living room. An arm's length of paperbacks—mostly Tom Clancy and the like—fit perfectly on a shelf over the TV. Magazines were fanned out across the coffee table—the *Independent Grocer* was one title she saw. There wasn't a speck of dust anywhere. She hadn't realized that Thaddeus was obsessively neat. Her first reaction was admiration—she loved seeing everything in its place—but when she considered the mind that kept everything so pristine, she had second thoughts. This apartment was empty of character, as neat and depressing as Dr. Hammond's waiting room before the first patient arrived in the morning.

Thaddeus dropped a shaving brush into the shoebox, explaining with a smile, "This is too stiff to use, but I can't bring myself to throw it away because it belonged to my dad." He added a ring and said, "That's it."

"That's all?" said Big Edna. She shook the box under his chin.

"It is." His wrinkled face took on its serious look. "And now if you'll excuse me, *Days of Our Lives* is about to come on."

"Well, he's probably like me," Big Edna said, leading the way to the opposite end of the corridor. "He wants to wait and see if the plan works before he puts in his really valuable stuff."

Following along, Agatha asked herself, as she did a hundred times a day, *What am I doing here?*

Big Edna stopped at the last room on the right, tried the door but it wouldn't open. Agatha was gratified to find at least one door locked besides her own. Big Edna knocked but got no response. "Well, that's mighty strange," she said. "Where is she?"

"Here I come," called a voice from behind them. It was a tall woman whose clothing Agatha had been admiring at every meal. Instead of the standard Sunset uniform—a pair of polyester slacks and a short-sleeved, flowered top with black or white ground-gripper shoes—today she wore a brown sweater over an attractive dark dress and expensive-looking shoes. So this must be Harriet Hillyard.

Agatha introduced herself and saw something very appealing in the woman's eyes, a sign of happiness, as if meeting Agatha caused her sincere pleasure. She said, "I feel I've known you all my life, Miss McGee; I've heard so much about you."

"What have you heard?" Agatha wanted to know.

"Well, let me see," said the woman with a laugh and a warm handshake. "I've heard you were a superb teacher in your day. The local Catholic school, I believe? And I've heard you were living on River Street until last week when you became our new woman. I'm so glad you moved in, because I've been known as the new woman for almost the past three months and now at last everybody has to call me by my name. Harriet. Harriet Hillyard."

Big Edna Brink stepped between them, rattling the shoebox in front of Harriet's nose. "Your valuables," she said.

She was not happy when Harriet said, "In a minute, Mrs. Brink," and continued talking to Agatha, telling her that she came from Rookery and had four children, the eldest of whom was named Jane, a doctor in Minneapolis. The second, Laurie, was teaching sixth grade at nearby Bartlett Elementary; and the third, she said in conclusion, was a research chemist named David at the University of Minnesota.

Agatha decided against asking about the fourth because she didn't want to upset Big Edna further, who was fuming at the waste of time. The group crowded into the Hillyard apartment, which was overcrowded with tastefully chosen furniture, while Harriet deposited something in the box. From where she stood, Agatha couldn't see what it was. She studied the framed photographs on the living room wall. All were of four rather long-haired young people, two girls and two boys.

"Me next," said Addie Greeno, and the group left the room, heading for the elevator. Before taking her leave, Agatha surprised herself by asking Harriet Hillyard if she'd like to come upstairs for tea sometime. The woman's response, "Oh, indeed I would. Just say when," prompted Agatha to specify the next morning. She returned upstairs with a high heart, feeling as if she'd just made a new friend.

Around ten o'clock the next morning, Agatha, expecting Harriet Hillyard, answered a knock and was then pulled suddenly out into the hallway by John Beezer, who grabbed her wrist. Breathless and frightened, she stood with her hand over her heart and said with as much sternness as she could muster, "Well, Mr. Beezer!"

"Just wanted you to try one of these here venison sticks," he said, looking at the floor as he handed her a thin stick of dried meat. It resembled a piece of the salted beef jerky that Frederick was fond of and sometimes brought home from the pool hall. "My boy Ernie shot a deer this fall," John Beezer added. "Big buck. See what you think of it."

She took it, thanking him, and waited for him to leave, which he seemed reluctant to do. He obviously expected her to taste it on the spot. "I will want to rinse it off before I bite into it," she explained.

"Rinse it off?" he said incredulously.

"Yes, of course. Now run along and I will give you my opinion at lunch."

Obediently he crossed the hall and stepped into the elevator.

A few minutes later, sitting at her kitchen table having tea with Harriet Hillyard, Agatha spoke of this strange encounter. "He's really quite frightening. As soon as I unlocked my door, he pulled me so hard I went flying out into the corridor."

"Yes, he's very awkward, but he's harmless," said her guest. "After I moved in, I had my daughter check up on him. She lives in Bartlett, you see, the town he comes from. He has a reputation for being very reclusive, but that's all. He farmed, you understand, and he missed out on the social graces. He was only married for a short time many years ago and his wife died in childbirth. So he has the one son, a man named Ernest, I believe, Ernest Beezer, who's still on the farm."

"That's all very well," said Agatha. "But I can't get it out of my head that he's a thief." She explained then about her lost brooch. "Who else, of all those living here, could have stolen it?" she asked.

"Big Edna Brink would be my candidate," said Harriet without hesitation.

Agatha considered this, and rejected it. "No, Big Edna came

in while I was here yesterday and you could tell by the way she looked around that she'd never seen the inside of this room before."

"Well, I only say that because she's such a pushy thing."

"And she'd have to have a key, because my door has always been locked."

"Oh, that wouldn't be a problem for Big Edna. I can imagine her somehow getting ahold of a master key and duplicating it."

"I see. Well, perhaps . . ." But Agatha had no intention of changing her mind. After a lifetime of studying the faces of students, she recognized guilt in John Beezer's habit of avoiding eye contact.

She brought to the table the stick of venison jerky, rinsed and cut in half, and offered half to her guest. "Here's what he brought me. He said it's made from a deer his son shot this fall."

"Oh, my goodness, no. The very idea of eating wild game makes my stomach upset. My late husband and our elder son used to hunt ducks and grouse and they'd urge me to try it, but I just couldn't. I couldn't even cook what they brought home."

"Well, I have a stomach as tough as a galvanized pail, and because I told him I'd let him know what I think of it . . ." Agatha picked up half the stick and bit into it. She chewed thoughtfully, then said, "Not half bad," and ate the other half as well.

"So, Miss McGee, what do you think of the shoebox making the rounds?"

"It was Lillian's idea, and because she's such an old friend I'm going along with it. I don't mind admitting that I'm surprised you're taking part."

"Yes, well, Big Edna said you were in on it, so I thought it was safe." She saw Agatha's surprise at this and added, "Oh yes, she made a great deal of your being part of the plan. You appear to be one of the few people she has respect for."

"But if you suspect her of thievery, how can you give her your valuables?"

"I didn't. I gave her an old billfold with nothing much in it. Two dollar bills and a bunch of old lottery tickets."

"Whose lottery tickets?" asked Agatha. Surely this impressive woman, dressed today in a dark blue pantsuit with an expensive-looking necklace at her throat, couldn't be a gambler.

"Mine," she answered. "I buy one or two a week, at a dollar apiece. Or if the jackpot is up over a hundred million, I'll buy half a dozen." Seeing a look of distaste on Agatha's face, she added, "Of course, you don't buy lottery tickets, do you, Miss McGee?"

"You can tell by looking at me?"

"I can tell by your reputation. I'd guess that you've never bought even one ticket in your life."

"You're right," said Agatha proudly. "I wouldn't know how to ask for one. Nor would I know what to do with a hundred million dollars."

"Nor would I, but what an exciting problem to have."

What a foolish attitude, thought Agatha, who had reached a point in her life where she hoped that every problem, exciting or not, was behind her. She shifted subjects, saying, "You said you had four children, one being a doctor in the Twin Cities—"

"Did I say four?"

"Yes, and one teaching in Bartlett and one a research chemist . . ."

Harriet Hillyard looked about her, squirming in her chair. "I said four out of habit. I must start saying three. I don't know why I'm telling you this, but my youngest son is . . ." Her voice broke and she backed up and came at it again. "I haven't told a soul in Staggerford about this, but my youngest son is . . . in prison."

Agatha handed her a Kleenex and she dabbed her eyes and continued. "He's been arrested countless times on drug charges, and last time he was sent to prison. He was our youngest and such a good boy growing up. We never saw this coming on." She wept copiously. "I'm just glad my husband didn't live to see it. The boy's name was Kirk."

Agatha urged, "Don't talk about him in the past tense unless he's dead. He's still your son after all."

At this, Harriet Hillyard stood up as though to leave. Agatha, regretting her advice, stood up as well, and when she did, her guest took her in her arms and embraced her tightly, stooping to do so because Agatha was considerably shorter. "Oh, Miss McGee, thank you for saying that. I've been so embarrassed; I've tried pretending that Kirk wasn't mine, but of course that hasn't been working." She sat again and so did Agatha. "It's the reason I've come to live here, because in Rookery everybody knew about Kirk and they seemed to blame me for it. At least my husband's family did, especially his mother. Yes, I still have a mother-in-law, Miss McGee; she'll be a hundred and one this winter, and she's decided she's going to her grave despising me."

She finished weeping and went on. "This place is pleasanter than I imagined it. I mean the town and my rooms and the meals. It's all very civilized except, of course, for Mr. Beezer and Edna Brink. I had a place lined up for myself in Rookery at Rookery Manor, very elegant apartments compared to these, but when I saw that I had to leave town to preserve my sanity, I chose Staggerford because it's only eight miles from my daughter in Bartlett. That's Laurie. She comes to see me every week. You'll have to meet her and compare teaching notes. I'll warn you ahead of time, she's quite heavy."

There was a knock on the door. Agatha opened it cautiously and found Lillian standing there with a toothbrush in her hand. "I just came to borrow a little toothpaste," she said coming in, and seeing Mrs. Hillyard, she added, "Don't pay any attention to me, you two, I'm just out of toothpaste."

Agatha turned and headed through her bedroom and toward her bathroom for a tube of Colgate, but Lillian called her back. "I'll just use a little bit off your wall." Agatha returned and found her looking closely at the white walls of the living room. Finding a scarcely noticeable dent above the TV, she swiped her toothbrush across it and hurried away.

"What a crazy idea!" said Harriet Hillyard, laughing.

Agatha, mystified and examining the dent, asked, "Do you understand what she did?"

"Oh yes." It took her a moment to catch her breath. "You see, it's well known that after a resident moves out, Little Edna Rinkwitz comes in and does up the apartment for the next one to move in, and one of the things she does is fill the nail holes on the walls where pictures hung with white toothpaste. But I've never known anybody to brush their teeth with it."

Agatha stepped back and saw several places on her walls where filler was slightly shinier than the flat paint. She thought, *No wonder everybody's walls are painted white.* She also thought, *I must tell Frederick about this trick,* but then realized that her rooms on River Street, even the bathroom and kitchen, were painted in colors no toothpaste could match.

Harriet Hillyard was still chuckling over what she called Lillian's ingenuity when she thanked Agatha for the tea and left.

Lillian's ingenuity? At least Agatha chose to believe it was that, instead of stupidity, which Harriet found so amusing. When they were girls in school, Lillian would embarrass Agatha by doing and saying dumb things. In fact, an occasional need to distance herself from Lillian had carried over into adulthood, until a priest pointed out in confession one day that if Lillian was a constant cause of this sin, it would be better if Agatha dissolved the friendship entirely. Which of course was out of the question. They lived across the alley from each other. They had been friends since they learned to talk. Agatha was actually frightened by the prospect of ignoring Lillian, of going through life without her. So from that day forward, instead of dissolving the relationship, she had stood by her friend through thick and thin.

Another knock at her door. "Who is it?" she called, busy clearing the table of tea things.

"It's day two, your turn," sang the husky voice of Big Edna Brink.

She opened the door and Big Edna thrust the shoebox at her, saying, "Sorry we can't stay. Me and Lillian are on our way to Kmart."

The shoe box was surprisingly heavy. Hefting it, Agatha experienced an unexpected feeling of responsibility. Here were the valuable and not-so-valuable things belonging to six people—money and rings and other jewelry as well as Lillian's partial roll of Tums. She wondered if the other five felt as she did, as though she'd been given a great trust. She took it to her bedroom and slipped it under her bed, then pulled the quilt over so that it hung down to the floor and hid the box. Later, returning from lunch, and then from supper, she went straight to her bedroom to make sure the box was still there.

7

What am I doing here? thought Agatha at eleven o'clock the next morning as she stood in Kmart's windy parking lot with Lillian, Big Edna Brink, Harriet Hillyard, Addie Greeno, and a few other townspeople Agatha didn't know. They were waiting for the bus to the Blue Sky Casino. Most of them were holding their lunches in paper bags. Agatha was bundled up in her engulfing down coat and hood, which left only two inches of her lower leg exposed to the elements. Waiting as well, though at some distance from the women, were Thaddeus Druppers and John Beezer. Thaddeus was reading a newspaper.

"You're sure the bus ride costs nothing?" Agatha said to Lillian.

"Not a cent."

"But how can the bus company afford it?"

"Search me."

Harriet Hillyard, overhearing, answered, "It's not a bus company bus; it's from the casino. You see, the aim is to get as many people gambling as possible. That way they take in more money."

The word *gambling* made Agatha think of a ratty bunch of poker players sitting at a round table in the smoky back room of some dive. She searched her memory in vain, trying to find the origin of this image, and decided it must have been a composite of movie scenes she'd watched on TV over the years. (She hadn't attended a movie theater since 1982, when Debra Winger, naked as a jaybird in *An Officer and a Gentleman*, crawled into bed with Richard Gere.)

The enormous silver bus that pulled into the parking lot was driven by a jolly man Agatha thought she recognized. He opened the door, tipped his hat and said, "Welcome, ladies." Seated behind the wheel, he spoke to each woman as she climbed aboard, making a joke about the weather or commenting on the handsome coat or scarf she wore. Agatha held up the line by saying, "I believe you are Gerald Bigmeadow." He had been one of the few Indian children to attend St. Isidore's.

"Yes, ma'am," he said, laughing. "You bet I am." Then, looking closer at her, he squealed "Miss McGee!" in a piercing falsetto, and rising from his place at the wheel, he ushered her to a seat about halfway back. "I never pegged you for a gambler, Miss McGee."

"You're right about that. I have never so much as—"

"You're going to have the time of your life," he broke in, patting her on the shoulder and then hurrying back to his seat.

As the bus pulled out of town, she heard Thaddeus Druppers in the seat behind her rattling his newspaper and complaining to John Beezer that the *Star Tribune* had changed the print in its TV log.

"Look at this page, John, who can read print this small?"

John Beezer coughed a deep bronchial cough and said, "They's more about the shows."

"I *know* there's more about the shows, but who cares what it says if you can't read it?"

"Print hasta be that small to make room."

"I'm going to write to the paper."

Lillian, with her bag of knitting in her lap, was sitting next to Agatha. "Did Big Edna come by for the shoebox this morning?" she asked.

"Yes, around nine o'clock."

"The reason I ask, she's not feeling the best. She's got a tooth abscess way back here." Lillian stuck her finger deep into her mouth to demonstrate.

"The poor woman," said Agatha, looking at Big Edna sitting ahead of her and across the aisle. She sat alone, for she took up more than her share of the two seats. "Why isn't she at the dentist?"

"Oh, she wouldn't miss her day at the casino for anything."

Seated in front of Agatha and Lillian were Harriet Hillyard and Addie Greeno. Harriet turned around and, nodding at Big Edna, she whispered loudly, "I don't believe she brought a lunch."

Bringing out her knitting, Lillian said, "She never does. She eats the casino's lunch."

"Why don't we all eat the casino's lunch?" asked Agatha.

"Cuz we save five bucks by bringing our own."

Then Agatha remembered that Lillian, who never gambled, made this weekly trip to Blue Sky Casino for the money. She'd told Agatha that the casino management gave each gambler a certain number of quarters to get them started, and Lillian always just brought hers home.

The bus went north to Willoughby, then took a westbound road Agatha had never seen before. It wound up and down over forested hills and skirted ponds that were frozen at the edges and reflected the white trunks of bare birches. The ride thrilled Agatha. It had been years since she'd left the city limits of Staggerford, and she reveled in the beauty of the sunny morning. *If the rest of the day proves a waste of time, as I believe it will, at least I have this,* she thought.

The bus pulled into a ten- or fifteen-acre parking lot holding perhaps four dozen cars and pickup trucks. Most were parked near a mammoth building, over the door of which red neon announced BLUE SKY CASINO and, underneath, SANDHILL OJIBWAY RESERVATION. Crossing from the bus to the building, Agatha was intrigued by a number of children playing outside a brand-new, windowless brick building with SANDHILL ELEMENTARY written across the front.

"My, how the reservation has changed since I was out here last," she said to Thaddeus walking at her side. "Sandhill Elementary used to be a miserable little building south of here, just west of Staggerford. It had outdoor toilets and I was told the roof leaked."

"Yes, things are looking up for the Indians ever since the casino came in. Their gambling profits built that school, and over there behind it"—he pointed—"is a great big motel. But it's a shame they don't straighten out the road from Willoughby."

"Oh, it's a beautiful drive," she said.

Ignoring her opinion, he said, "A decent road in here would double the number of people, I'm sure. But look at this beautiful parking lot, would you." They turned and looked back the way they had come. Thaddeus spread his arms to indicate the acres of blacktop with a thousand yellow lines painted on it. He sighed like a man who's just been granted a glimpse of paradise and said, "All that tar!"

It was a slow day at the casino, which meant there were only forty or fifty people playing the gambling machines, which stretched away as far as Agatha could see. The red and green neon made it seem as bright as outdoors, but it took a minute for her eyes to adjust to it. She stood in line to check her coat and receive a half a roll of quarters from the second Indian she recognized that morning—Beverly Bingham Mulholland, the daughter of a murderer, and now the wife of Staggerford's mayor, both of whom had helped her out the day her pipes froze.

"Beverly, I didn't know you worked here."

"I fill in when people are gone," she said, not looking up at first from her tray of coins, but when she did, she exclaimed, "Agatha McGee!" and, setting down her tray, put her arms around her, but very carefully, for Agatha was quite small and fragile.

They discussed the water pipes in Agatha's house for a minute, and then Beverly launched into a lengthy account of her son Owen's troubles caused by alcohol and manic depression. That fall Owen had belatedly enrolled in college—he was twenty-seven—but seldom attended classes and was on probation and about to be expelled, and today he was in jail, having been arrested for reckless driving. "But Agatha, what about you? What brings you to Blue Sky? You're the last person I ever expected to see at a casino."

As Beverly led her here and there, showing her the various gambling machines, Agatha explained how her friends at Sunset Senior Apartments had prevailed upon her to come and see what the casino was like that she'd heard so much about—from Lillian mostly. She went on to say that in years past she'd never have made this trip for fear of causing scandal—she'd always followed the straight and narrow path as an example to her fellow townsmen—but since moving into her apartment she had realized how drastically she and the town had changed. "There are fewer eyes on me these days, Beverly, because Staggerford is populated with strangers."

Why am I telling this to Beverly? she wondered. *What am I doing here?* She thanked Beverly for the tour and went and sat in an easy chair beside Lillian, who was knitting. She was facing the bent backs of three elderly gamblers—two women and a man—sitting on high stools and putting coins in the machines Beverly had called one-armed bandits. They pulled levers that caused pictures of cherries and apples and such to spin on the screen. Suddenly a bell in the machine in front of one of the elderly women began to ring—a furious clanging noise that caused Lillian to look up from the garment she was making. The woman held a plastic bucket under a spout and out came a pile of coins. The clanging stopped. Agatha expected her to shout or exult in some way, but she seemed unmoved. The old man sitting next to her made some comment, but she ignored it and went on putting coins in the machine. Agatha wished she was acquainted with the woman so that she could go over and tell her to quit, to go home while she was ahead.

In a few minutes the other woman hit a jackpot, but a smaller one—her winnings she caught in her hands, which she held under the spout. She, too, ignored a comment from the old man and continued feeding coins into the slot.

After a time, Agatha heard in the distance the excited cry of a big winner, along with a machine chiming away as it poured out coins. "I won, I won, I won," was the cry, and it drew closer until around the corner, and heading straight for Agatha came John Beezer at a run. "Mrs. McGee, look at this!" he said, thrusting forward his plastic bucket for her inspection. He then dug a hand into the bucket and said, "Put out your hands," and when she did so, he poured twenty or thirty quarters into them and scampered away.

"What was that all about?" said Lillian, glancing suspiciously at Agatha.

"That's what I'd like to know."

"Maybe he's sweet on you. Stranger things have happened, you know."

"Heaven forbid."

After eating her peanut butter and banana sandwich—a combination she'd recently become addicted to—Agatha dozed in her chair for a time and then, seeing that she had about an hour until bus time, she stepped up to a one-armed bandit and slipped one of the coins Beverly had given her into its slot. The pictures of vegetables and fruit spun to no avail. She put in another coin. Again nothing. She did this a total of five times and gave up. Returning to her chair, she found that Lillian had been replaced by Thaddeus, who was addressing a postcard. He asked Agatha if she had a stamp.

"Back at the apartment, but not with me, I'm afraid."

"Here, read this," he said. "See if there's anything wrong with it."

She took the card with its photograph of the casino and read a note of complaint to the *Minneapolis Star Tribune* in Thaddeus's sketchy but neat hand concerning its small print in the TV log. "It's fine," she said, handing it back to him, "except you don't connect your letters very well."

"But the content, Agatha, what about what I said. Is it clear enough?"

"It is, Thaddeus." She didn't add that she was disappointed in him. She hadn't realized he was such a fussbudget. She pulled up a folding chair and sat down close to him. "Thaddeus, what's got into John Beezer? Just a few minutes ago, he gave me part of his winnings."

"John Beezer considers you a friend, ever since you asked him where he came from the other night at dinner."

"Oh? And what was so remarkable about that?"

"I guess it was remarkable to John. Nobody ever talks to him, you see. Not women anyway. I do, of course, but that doesn't count." Thaddeus rose from his chair. "Have you had any luck here today?"

"No, I've lost a dollar and a quarter."

As departure time drew near, Beverly Mulholland came back and sat down next to Agatha. "Now that you've broken the ice, I hope you'll come back again."

"Not soon. Maybe someday, to win back the dollar and a quarter I lost."

8

The next afternoon, at the weekly Friday coffee hour, Agatha met several visitors to Sunset Senior, including Harriet Hillyard's daughter the teacher. She was enormous, as Harriet had warned, even heavier than Big Edna Brink, and she wore jeans and a sweatshirt. She had attractive auburn hair.

"No school today?" asked Agatha.

"Oh, sure, but I cut out early," said Miss Hillyard, taking a seat across the table from Agatha.

Agatha resisted the temptation to ask if she'd changed clothes before driving over from Bartlett, or if jeans were now an acceptable getup for a teacher. In Agatha's day at St. Isidore's Elementary, jeans had been forbidden across the board, even for the children.

It turned out that Laurie Hillyard taught sixth grade, just as Agatha had done, but they had little in common. Agatha was shocked to hear that Laurie's students had no assigned desks but sat where they wished each day, perhaps on the floor, sometimes on windowsills. She had one hyperactive student, in fact, who never sat anywhere, but kept moving around the room and even *out* of the room and down the corridor while Laurie tried to teach.

"Goodness," said Agatha, "I retired just in time." She described her classroom at St. Isidore's with its neat rows of desks bolted to the floor and each child in his or her place throughout the year—until the day each spring when, as a special reward for behaving like ladies and gentlemen, she allowed her students to change places and sit anywhere they wished for one hour.

"Yes, I've heard of the old days when students were regimented like that," said Laurie. "There are still classrooms like that in high school but not in elementary."

"You mean they spend six years in such chaos?"

"Seven in Bartlett, including kindergarten. It's so they don't grow up feeling restricted, so they can be unfettered and think for themselves."

Agatha felt a hand laid roughly on her shoulder. It was John Beezer standing behind her and introducing his son. "Here's the new woman I told you about, Ernie, the one I give the stick of venison to." The young man was a carbon copy of his father— wild bushy hair, dark hooded eyes, a prominent nose. "Nice t'meetcha," he said.

"Likewise, I'm sure." She took the calloused hand he offered and saw that Ernie, like his father, would not look her in the eye.

As she turned back to Laurie Hillyard to say that too much freedom wasn't good for youngsters, she was aware of the two Beezers continuing to stand behind her.

"Oh, I agree with you completely," said Laurie. "The question is how much is too much freedom."

Again the hand on her shoulder. "She's the one asked me about the farm," John Beezer said to his son. Then with his mouth close to Agatha's ear, he asked confidentially, "Missus, do you garden?"

"I used to garden. I haven't for many years."

"Well, come spring, Ernie here's going to bring his rototiller and plow us up a garden in the front yard."

"You'd better check with Edna Rinkwitz about that."

"Yeah, Ernie already did. She said it was okay if enough people wanted to garden. I'll put your name down."

At this point, Addie Greeno came over to Agatha's table

leading a middle-aged man by the hand and introduced him as her son, Harold. "You remember Agatha McGee, Harold, she was once your teacher, wasn't she?"

"I believe so, yes," he said, taking her hand and giving her a formal little bow. "How are you, Ms. McGee?"

"Harold Greeno," said Agatha. "I've often wondered what became of you. You were living on the West Coast, last I heard. I remember your being our milk monitor in grade six, and also what a whiz you were at kickball."

"Oh, I was, was I?" He laughed an embarrassed laugh and looked about as though he was afraid someone might be overhearing Agatha's memories of thirty years ago. "I got my law degree and live in Salem, Oregon."

"He's a lawyer," said Addie proudly, "and he's had two wives."

Agatha introduced Harold Greeno to Thaddeus, who sat on her right. "He was the only grocer in town in your day; remember, Harold?"

"Oh, he was, was he?" Harold Greeno said vaguely, obviously recalling very little of his childhood.

"Say, I've got a question for all of you," said Thaddeus Druppers. "I got it out of a magazine. Imagine that you overhear somebody on the street tell somebody else that it's a quarter after six. Now the question is, what do you do? Do you (a) take that person's word for it, or (b) look at your watch to check the time yourself, or (c) ignore the whole deal and get on about your business?"

John Beezer, having sat down on Agatha's left, answered immediately, "I'd take his word for it; why not?" while everyone else looked thoughtful.

Why not? Because it was no good trusting the word of a stranger, thought Agatha. She knew her answer—she would check her watch—but she wanted to know the consequences of revealing this before speaking out. "What do our answers mean?" she asked Thaddeus.

"Well, John's answer means he's a trusting fellow," he replied. "If your answer is that you'd ignore the whole deal, then you're highly motivated."

"And if you'd check your watch?"

"You're probably paranoid."

"Well," said Agatha, glancing at her watch, "It's exactly ten to four."

Thaddeus and Laurie Hillyard looked at their watches. The rest of those within earshot simply nodded.

Laughing bitterly, she said, "At least I'm not the only one."

Little Edna, having provided everyone with a piece of cake and ice cream, quieted the crowd and announced that someone had lost a shoe, someone else had lost an umbrella and still someone else had lost a valuable brooch. Finders please return these items to her office.

Agatha saw that John Beezer's face betrayed nothing at the mention of the brooch—probably because he didn't know the meaning of the word, she thought.

"Childhood is a time for freedom," said Laurie Hillyard, continuing their earlier conversation. "You can't rein in a child's spirit and expect him to grow into a responsible citizen."

Thaddeus said, "You see, the question about looking at your watch is really a psychological test, don't you know. It gets to the heart of who you really are."

Harold Greeno told Agatha that he had earned his law degree at the University of Minnesota. "I bet you never thought I'd amount to a hill of beans, did you, Ms. McGee?"

John Beezer told her that he hoped she was fond of cosmos because he had a lot of cosmos seeds left over from last summer and intended to plant all of them in front of the apartment building.

Addie Greeno said, "Harold used to be married to a woman with two kids, and another woman with one kid, and he's lucky to be shut of both of them, but his monthly alimony bills are sky-high."

Ernie Beezer, sitting beside his father, said the first of May was a good time to till the soil.

All of these remarks seemed to be directed at Agatha, but she responded to none of them. She was planning her return to her house on River Street. Tomorrow she'd have given this place a week—long enough. Tomorrow was Frederick's day off from the mail route. She'd call him and ask him to come help her pack and whisk her away. Because she didn't belong here. What had she accomplished in her week under this roof? She'd gone to the Blue Sky Casino, and she'd played at a game Lillian made up called the MX Shoebox. That was it. That's all she'd done.

John Beezer said he had it in mind to put in a bunch of phlox because phlox kept coming back year after year. Purple was his favorite color for phlox. Harold Greeno said Oregon was paradise, while his mother said he'd sworn off women entirely after two bad marriages. Thaddeus said there was a lot you could tell about people from the way they answered questions like what would you do if you heard somebody tell somebody else what time it was. Ernie Beezer said he'd have to check the blades on his rototiller and make sure they were sharp enough to turn up new ground. Laurie Hillyard gave her mother a peck on the cheek, stood up, and said good-bye. She had an appointment in Bartlett and had to get back.

With her mind on her move, Agatha gave Miss Hillyard an absent nod of farewell. Agatha carried around an image of herself living in her big house on River Street, and she believed everyone else did the same. Thaddeus—and there was no telling how many others—had been surprised to find her living here. Agatha hated surprising people. All her life she'd striven to be

predictable. It was too bad she'd ever made this move. She'd
been weak and all coughed out when she allowed Lillian and her
other friends to talk her into it.

Thaddeus, too, got up to leave, promising Agatha another
psychological test tomorrow at lunch. John Beezer said, "Good-
bye, Missus," and followed his son out of the room. Addie
Greeno led her son to another table and introduced him as a
man with two divorces to his credit.

Agatha continued to sit, realizing that her main reason for
leaving was that she detested living among thieves. Somebody
had stolen her diamond brooch. She hated to leave here without
it. The brooch was her link with her father and mother. But it
wasn't her only one. The house itself was a link, and every piece
of furniture in it.

She was brought out of her thoughts by Harriet, who sat at
the far end of Agatha's table and asked how she liked Laurie.
"She's quite a girl, isn't she?"

"Yes," said Agatha, "quite a girl all right. But her manner of
teaching is a far cry from the way I used to do it."

"Yes, I noticed you were impressed with the freedom her
students have in the classroom."

"Did you learn that way?"

"No, of course not," said Harriet Hillyard. "It's the new
thinking."

"It's the return of the Dark Ages," said Agatha.

They left the coffee hour together. Agatha surprised Harriet
by passing up the elevator and accompanying her down the corridor. "I'm looking for 120," said Agatha.

"Oh, 120 is across from me, down at the end," Harriet said,
then added with a distasteful look, "But that's John Beezer's
apartment."

Harriet waited while Agatha knocked, but just before the
door was opened by Ernie Beezer, she fled into her apartment.

"Is your father here?" asked Agatha.

"Yeah, but he's in the can." At six foot three or four, Ernie towered over her.

She heard a toilet flush and John Beezer stepped into the living room tightening his belt. He didn't notice Agatha until his son said, "It's the new woman, Dad."

An immediate expression of delight crossed his face, but was quickly replaced by a frown of disappointment when Agatha said, "Mr. Beezer, did you steal my brooch?"

"Your what?" he asked.

"My brooch. A pin for wearing on my blouse or lapel. It's in the shape of a bow and studded with diamonds."

"No, Missus."

"Hey, what's the idea of accusing my dad of robbery?" said his son.

"Do you have a master key, Mr. Beezer?"

"A master key? What's that?"

"A key to everyone's apartment."

"Hey, what's the idea?" Ernie repeated.

"I don't have no master key, Missus."

Ernie took a step toward her, so she pulled the door shut and hurried upstairs, thinking that John Beezer's denial had been so convincing she was almost sorry she'd confronted him. There was no guile in the man, no capacity for tricking her into believing him innocent, but then who had taken the brooch?

No one, she discovered when she began folding her shirts and blouses in preparation for tomorrow's move. For there on the blue shirt she'd worn last Saturday, right where she'd pinned it before leaving her house, was the diamond brooch.

9

Agatha checked her list of Christmas dinner guests again and again to make sure she'd left out none of her friends. Frederick, as usual, had declined to invite his friends from Kruger's Pool Hall, where he liked to spend his days off from work. When she asked him why, he'd only shrugged, but as he told Lee Ann Raft (whom he *did* invite) one morning along his mail route, none of his pool hall buddies were the type of people Agatha would approve of. Lee Ann was sitting in the backseat of his Oldsmobile handing the mail to him as he stopped at each mailbox. "I mean Christmas dinner at our house is a pretty high-toned affair," he said. "Mostly old ladies from Sunset Senior and Father Healy and people like that. Can you imagine somebody like Ernie Beezer sitting down to a meal with that crowd?"

No, she couldn't, but the picture of it in her mind caused her to laugh merrily. This was one of the things about Lee Ann Raft that Frederick liked most—how he could make her laugh so easily. It was a high-pitched, full-throated laugh and quite infectious. He chuckled along with her, imagining Ernie Beezer, who quite often drove over from Bartlett for lunch at Kruger's, belching and eating with his mouth open at Agatha's table.

That's why they were so shocked when Ernie Beezer, trailing his old father behind him, was the first guest to arrive at Agatha's house for Christmas dinner. Because Agatha, with Lillian, was busy in the kitchen, Frederick and Lee Ann stood arm in arm at the front door, playing host and hostess, and welcomed them into the living room. The Beezers each wore a clean pair of overalls. They sat some distance apart, Ernie sinking into the couch and putting his feet up on a hassock, while his father sat alertly on the edge of a straight chair, looking about him like a bird on a branch. Evidently he found Agatha's furnishings to his liking because he said, "Ain't bad, huh, Ernie?"

"Sure 'nuff," said Ernie, digging himself deeper into the couch. "Pretty spiffy all right."

Lee Ann asked Ernie how he knew Agatha.

"Dad knows her from Sunset Senior. Guess she invited him and he invited me."

His father spoke up, explaining, "I told Missus McGee I usually take Christmas dinner with my son, and rather than leave him alone, she said to bring him along." He studied Frederick for a minute, then asked him, "How do *you* know her?"

"She's my great-aunt," he said. Then he went on to say, "Lee Ann brought her father last year for the same reason. Her sister Karen got married the summer before, and her other sister, Janet, and her family were out of town, so he'd have been alone too."

Ernie said to his father, "That's Francis Raft they're talking about. You knew him."

John Beezer's eyes lit up momentarily. "Francis Raft . . . I knew him. I bought hay from him a time or two. But he's dead, ain't he?"

Lee Ann said yes, her father had died the previous spring of lung cancer. "Smoked like a chimney all his life," she added.

John Beezer said, "I smoked till ten years ago; got so short of breath I quit. Still do miss a cigarette now and again."

"Either of you guys smoke?" asked Ernie.

"Once in a while I'll take a few drags," said Lee Ann. "When I can bum a cigarette off somebody."

"I don't smoke," said Frederick, ashamed, for some reason,

to admit it. He remembered his buddies in Vietnam smoking all kinds of stuff—marijuana and opium as well as tobacco—and he didn't know why he'd never joined in. Maybe it was because of how sick he got in high school the time he'd tried a cigar. It had been the year his dad died. He was in Mercy Hospital wasting away with a serious heart condition, and Frederick would drop in to see him every day after school. One day a man who'd just become a father was handing out cigars, and he gave one to Frederick, who at sixteen was tall for his age and could have been mistaken for an adult.

He wanted to light up in the hospital parking lot, but he didn't have a match, so he waited until he got home. It must have been a Monday because that was the day his mother was late getting home from cleaning people's houses. He sat at the kitchen table and smoked very little of the cigar before running to the bathroom and throwing up. His mistake was that in trying to inhale he'd swallowed a lot of smoke. For hours afterward he was so sick he wanted to die.

Next through the door came the party of Agatha's friends from Sunset Senior. Big Edna, Addie, Harriet, and her large daughter. "Hello, Addie," Frederick said to the only one of the four he knew. Agatha came in from the kitchen and introduced the others. "And this is Lee Ann Raft," she concluded, "Frederick's fiancée." Frederick saw Lee Ann flinch and blush at this, but bless her, she didn't protest. She knew Agatha well enough to realize that "engaged" was the only way she could think about a man and a woman who saw so much of each other. Shaking the hands of the four women, he realized that the sizes of Edna Brink and Laurie Hillyard would make it very crowded at the twelve closely set places in the dining room.

He noticed too that Agatha didn't look well. He'd never before seen her looking so drawn and pale. This dinner had exhausted her, and it was just beginning. From his room upstairs he'd heard her up half the night, setting the table and getting pots and pans ready in the kitchen. He'd wanted to tell her, *You're too old to throw a big party anymore, Agatha. Give it a rest. You haven't got the stamina for it.* But of course that would have made her only more determined, so he confined his admonition to the number of guests. This morning, when he'd seen twelve places set at the table, he said, "You've got to cut down at your age, Agatha, instead of adding more and more. You were down to eight at Thanksgiving and so I thought—"

She surprised him by agreeing. She said, "I suppose you're right, Frederick. But the number of lonely hearts seems to grow by the year." She said this as she went around the table straightening the silver at each setting. "Or at least I've met more of them since Thanksgiving. It was that week at the Sunset Senior Apartments that did it. Six or seven of them are coming. But don't worry. After this is over I'm going to bed for a week."

Next to arrive was Father Healy, with whom Agatha had been on the outs more than once about matters of theology and liturgy. The latest trouble between them had to do with the remodeling of St. Isidore's Church. Father Healy was about to move the altar from its place at the front of the church down to the center of the congregation, and bring the organ and the choir down from the choir loft and put them in the empty sanctuary. It all seemed to Agatha like a blasphemous and unnecessary use of church property—for one thing, the priest, no matter which way he turned, would present his back to part of the congregation—and she led a movement of parishioners against the new design. She and her cohorts placed ads of protest in the *Staggerford Weekly* and later laminated them and posted them in the vestibule of the church and on nearby power poles. It was a useless effort. Father Healy polled the parish, and the protesters lost by five hundred votes.

Father Healy was a hugger of people he'd met before. He hugged Agatha, Frederick and Addie. He hugged Lee Ann, whom he remembered from Agatha's Thanksgiving dinner, and he shook the hands of the others. John Beezer mumbled, "Pleased t'meetcha," but his son said nothing, didn't even stand up when the priest took his hand. He only stared, as if fascinated by this stranger in a Roman collar and black suit—an outfit Father Healy wouldn't have worn to anyone's house but Agatha's.

Last to arrive was Imogene Kite, Lillian's unmarried fifty-six-year-old daughter and head librarian of the local Carnegie Library. She let everyone know what a vile mood she was in by greeting no one and pressing Father Healy firmly away from her when he stepped up to embrace her. Agatha wasn't surprised. Lillian, while working in the kitchen, had warned Agatha that Imogene was "not feeling the best." It was Frederick's fault, she explained, for he had chosen Lee Ann Raft as his girlfriend instead of Imogene.

Agatha placed Frederick and Lee Ann and the three women who made up the Sunset Senior delegation on one side of the table and Imogene, the Beezers and Laurie Hillyard on the other, leaving a place for Lillian on that side because it was closest to the kitchen. Father Healy she placed at the head of the table and herself at the foot. Everyone stood expectantly at their places for a minute until Father Healy concluded a prayer and the kitchen door swung open and Lillian entered bearing a ham and sweet potatoes on a platter, which caused them all to break into excited chatter.

"What a delicious dinner, Miss McGee," said Father Healy, and everyone agreed.

"Tell that to Lillian," said Agatha. "She's the cook."

Laurie Hillyard, not understanding the extent of Imogene's bitterness, tried to draw her out. "What's your most popular book at the library these days?"

"Trash," Imogene shot back. "About the only thing people read anymore is trash."

"The ham is from Druppers's, the butcher," said Lillian. "You can always count on Druppers's for good meat."

"But it isn't called Druppers's anymore," Agatha reminded her. "It's called Hawkins's, remember?"

"Oh, that reminds me, where is Thaddeus?" asked Lillian. "He was here for Thanksgiving."

"He's down with the flu. And so is my neighbor Linda Schwartzman. She was here at Thanksgiving too." Agatha thought, but didn't say, how timely their illnesses were. She couldn't have fit two more people around this table.

"You have such a lovely house," said Harriet. "So many nice things."

"Yeah, you sure have," said Big Edna who sat beside her. "But it's kind of bare. You've got lots of room for more knick-knack shelves. We ought to bring her some craft stuff from Little Edna's class, huh, Lillian?"

"No, Agatha wouldn't appreciate any of those things." Lillian was well acquainted with Agatha's abstemious taste, which she thought very strange. Strange, too, was how little Agatha was eating today. She usually ate like a horse, but today she was picking at her food. "Aren't you feeling good?" Lillian asked her.

"Shush, Lillian." Agatha was listening to John Beezer's account of the death of his wife, Essie. It happened when Ernie was a baby. Ernie had had a bad cold and the doctor was summoned out to the farm, and while he was tending to the baby, Essie sat down in a chair and died. "Just like that," he said with his mouth full of ham. "One minute she was fine; the next minute she was gone."

"But I understood she died in childbirth," said Harriet.

"Yeah, I don't know where that got started. Ernie was about a month old. Essie had a stroke or a heart attack or something and died right in the chair." He gave his son, who was hunched over his plate, a pat on the back and said, "So Ernie grew up without a mother, but he turned out okay anyhow. I don't know what I woulda done on the farm all those years without him. Why, he was drivin' the tractor from the time he was nine."

"I was seven," said Ernie, raising his head and looking proudly around the table.

Agatha was moved by John Beezer's story, by the bond between father and son, by the thought of these two men going through life on their own. She was moved as well by the thought that because of his rough edges, the father had been ostracized at Sunset Senior, and that she herself, by inquiring about his farm, had made him a devoted friend. She had apologized for accusing him of stealing her brooch, and he'd said, "Think nothing of it, Missus." On the day she moved back to her house, he had insisted on helping Frederick carry all her belongings down to the car and trailer. He wouldn't let Agatha lift a finger. The only thing she carried was her purse (with her brooch inside), and she sat in the lobby waiting until her apartment was empty and the little trailer was full of her furniture: her kitchen table and chairs, her TV and its stand, her rocking chair. Several of her friends, including Thaddeus and the Rinkwitzes, turned up in the lobby to bid her farewell, but John Beezer did them one better by standing outside the front door of Sunset Senior, waving as Frederick pulled away, and Agatha had waved back and impulsively—what had gotten into her?—thrown him a kiss.

Agatha hadn't told the women from Sunset Senior that she'd invited John Beezer today, because they might not have come. Addie certainly would have refused. As it was, she was eating with her left elbow on the table and her hand forming a hood over her eyes so she didn't have to see the Beezers chewing with their mouths open.

Lillian was concerned about Agatha's nibbling only a little of the food on her plate. And she looked so tired. To test her reactions, she said to Father Healy, "So how 'bout remodeling the church, Father? Aren't you about ready to start?" This topic would surely bring out Agatha's reactionary views.

"Yes," said the priest, "The day after Epiphany we're going

to go to work." He steeled himself for Agatha's response, but she didn't rise to the bait.

Lillian was alarmed. She said, "Agatha, why don't you go and lie down for half an hour. I'll keep your food warm."

Her guests were amazed when she said, "I believe I will," and she stood up, apologized, and groped her way into her bedroom, which was off the dining room, and closed the door. Everyone at the table fell silent. Frederick and Lillian exchanged a look that said they sensed this was the last of Agatha's holiday dinners for lonely hearts.

Agatha had never felt such fatigue. She lay down on top of her quilt, threw an afghan over herself and slept for two hours. She awoke to hear dishwashing noises and voices in the kitchen, then fell immediately back into a deep sleep. An hour later she awoke to silence. She felt much better. She got up and stretched. She was herself again.

She was surprised to find her guests gone. She went into the living room expecting to see Lillian dozing or knitting in her favorite chair, but the room was empty. She climbed halfway upstairs and heard snoring emanating from Frederick's room, so she knew he was napping. Where was Lillian? It wasn't like her to leave without waking Agatha and saying good-bye. She went back through the dining room and into the kitchen and found Lillian lying on the floor, next to the sink. Agatha, in her eighty-seven years, had learned to recognize death when she saw it. Her shout woke Frederick, who came hurrying downstairs.

10

The cause of death was a massive heart attack. The Sunset Senior Apartments emptied out for the funeral. Most of the residents walked to the church, since it was only a block and a half away, but Thaddeus drove because he was expected to take a carload of mourners to the cemetery after Mass. He went very early, as was his habit, and was surprised to find the hearse already parked in front of St. Isidore's. He pulled up immediately behind it so as to be first in line.

He considered leaving the MX Shoebox in his locked car, but decided to carry it into church to make sure nobody stole it. He'd brought it along because he had lost the key to his room and therefore left it unlocked. He would stash it somewhere in church, perhaps under a back pew during the funeral Mass. In the vestibule he found himself alone with the mortician and Lillian's body. The coffin was open for viewing. He stood and stared at Lillian until he heard the voices of other mourners entering behind him—Addie's high-pitched whine and Big Edna's big rumble. Thaddeus didn't like these two women, was actually afraid of them, Addie being such a complainer about her housemates and Big Edna being so gruff and high-handed concerning the MX Shoebox. "Make sure nobody gets ahold of this," she'd told him this morning when she brought it to his room. "We've been at it three weeks now, and we haven't lost it yet." Surely Big Edna would come down hard on him if she saw the shoebox under his arm, so he put it in the coffin with Lillian, pushing it down under the closed lower lid. He would retrieve it later, before the coffin was closed for the final time. But as more and more townspeople arrived he got caught up in various conversations and forgot about the box.

Agatha was dropped off at the church by Frederick. His substitute mail carrier was under the weather, so he couldn't attend Lillian's funeral. It was at the funeral that Agatha realized she wouldn't be able to stay in her house. Lillian had come in almost every day to dust, vacuum, and wash the dishes as if it were her own house. She changed the bed linens and took out the garbage. She worked as though all these household chores, which Agatha found so onerous, were second nature to her. Of course there were people who advertised for such work in the *Weekly*, but how could you relate to a stranger the way Agatha had related to Lillian?

Following the coffin out of St. Isidore's and riding to the cemetery in Thaddeus's shiny black Mercury, along with two or three other mourners, she remembered Lillian as a girl. Lily she was called in those days. She was almost exactly Agatha's age, having been born five days earlier, on September twenty-fifth. She had always been bigger and chunkier than Agatha, more physically fit, more athletic. Although Agatha was captain of the Girls' Athletic Association during her last two years in high school, it was Lillian who was always the high scorer in girls' basketball games, who won the blue ribbons at girls' track meets. Till the day she died, Lillian had followed the Minnesota Vikings on TV, while Agatha didn't know a quarterback from a goalpost.

Following the coffin across the snowy humps and hollows of the cemetery west of town, Agatha recalled that Lillian had not had an easy time of it academically. She remembered the difficulty Lillian had had as a first grader in memorizing the

Apostles' Creed. She remembered the time in the second grade when they had the word *basement* on their spelling list. When Sister Charles asked for a definition of the word, Lillian had raised her hand and said it was something they used in playing baseball. Throughout their school days they had studied together, one evening at Agatha's house, the next at Lillian's across the alley.

Standing at the foot of the grave while Father Healy read the Prayer of Burial, Agatha studied Lillian's daughter Imogene, who had been dry eyed throughout the ceremony. There was no reading the mind of Imogene Kite. Agatha remembered how she herself had gone off to college while Lillian married Lyle Kite right out of high school. It was twelve years later that Lillian gave birth to Imogene, their only child. From the start, in Agatha's opinion, Imogene had been a temperamental brat, a changeling unlike either of her parents. Lyle, a tall, quiet, unassuming man, had been a park ranger. He died suddenly just a few days after he retired. Lillian, who had been a widow for more than twenty years, had the most generous heart Agatha had ever known.

Watching Lillian's remains (and although she didn't know it, the MX Shoebox) lowered into her grave beside Lyle's, Agatha wept, regretting never telling Lillian how she valued her friendship. Driving back into town, Thaddeus tried to say comforting things until Agatha shut him up by exclaiming, "Death is a flaw in God's plan!" Her deep sadness was covered up by her anger.

When he pulled up in front of the church to partake of the lunch the Funeral Kitchen Committee had prepared, Agatha asked him to drive her the block and a half to the Sunset Senior Apartments. After letting out his other passengers, he did so, regaling her with a diatribe against Father Healy because he had failed to genuflect after the Consecration. "You of all people, Agatha, you've noticed how he never goes down on his knee at the Elevation, how he just gives a little bow of his head. Well, that's out-and-out blasphemy, Agatha. A priest is supposed to genuflect after he elevates both the bread *and* the wine. I'm going to write to the bishop about this, Agatha, mark my words."

Agatha said nothing. She didn't tell Thaddeus it was useless to appeal to Bishop Baker, because she'd seen Bishop Baker do the same thing at Mass. She resisted telling Thaddeus what a small-minded man he was. After all, she'd have to live with him in the same building until one of them died. When he pulled into Sunset Senior's circular drive, she asked him to wait for her, this would take only a minute.

"Better make it snappy," he said. "We don't want to miss lunch."

Opening the front door, Agatha was struck by the familiar smell of the place, a mixture of coffee and floor wax. Finding Edna Rinkwitz in her office, she announced her return to Sunset Senior. She said that because she had paid a month's rent when she moved in less than a month ago, she expected her same apartment back, overlooking Main Street.

"No, there's somebody else in that apartment," said Edna. "A Mrs. Teague moved in ten days ago."

"But that's *my* apartment! You still have my rent money."

"You forfeited your rent money when you moved out, Miss McGee."

"Do you mean my name now goes on the bottom of your waiting list?"

"Well, I suppose, since you were here once before, I can let you have Lillian Kite's apartment, once it's cleaned. Say New Year's Day?"

"I'll take it."

"Take me home," she told Thaddeus. She was angrily calculating how much of her money had gone toward Mrs. Teague's lodging.

"But you haven't had lunch," said Thaddeus.

"I don't want lunch."

"You don't want chili? It's chili. I smelled chili from the kitchen during the funeral."

"Chili gives me gas," she said, and asked him again to drive her home.

Four days later Agatha attended the funeral of Thaddeus Druppers at St. Isidore's. He had died, she was told, shortly after the lunch following Lillian's funeral. Addie Greeno said he'd acted very agitated while eating his bowl of chili and he left the church lunchroom in a hurry. He was found dead in his car in front of the Sunset Senior Apartments.

11

Agatha chose Thaddeus's apartment on the first floor, rather than Lillian's upstairs. Soon after moving in, she went upstairs and paid a visit to Mrs. Teague in her apartment over the front entrance. Mrs. Teague, a short, stout woman a few years younger than Agatha, proved to be friendly and talkative. After recounting her life story, she inquired about Agatha's. And so, beginning with her friendship with Lillian, Agatha spoke of her girlhood until she realized that Mrs. Teague wasn't listening. As soon as she stopped speaking, Mrs. Teague said there was a doctor coming to Sunset Senior that afternoon.

"Who?" asked Agatha. "Surely you don't mean Dr. Hammond. He never makes house calls."

"I don't know who. All I heard was that Dr. So-and-So will be down in the lobby at two o'clock." Mrs. Teague continued on with a tiresome recital of medical problems, her own and her late husband's. After several minutes of enlarged adenoids and swollen ankles, Agatha stood up and went to the window. She considered this front-and-center apartment, which everyone seemed to covet when she had lived here, actually inferior to her own because it faced north. She preferred the south because she liked the sun. Never mind the dismal view across the alley—the Dumpster behind Hawkins's Grocery, the beer trucks continually pulling up behind the liquor store—

the sun came flooding into her living room every day like a blessing.

Mrs. Teague had moved on from illness to death. "And wasn't it a shame about Mr. Druppers's suicide?"

"Thaddeus? You don't mean Thaddeus."

"Oh yes, did himself in. Gassed himself in his car. Old Beezer found him." She came over and stood beside Agatha at the window, pointing at the three or four cars parked on the circular drive. "Right down here in front. Had himself a hose attached to the tailpipe and the other end in through the back window. Left a note. I seen it. He wrote it on a postcard from the Blue Sky Casino."

"What did it say?"

"Most of it didn't make any sense to me. It was all about some lunch box or other. But at the end he said, 'Please mail this other card.' See, he had another postcard with the same picture on it of the casino already written to somebody and it was stamped and ready to go."

"Who was it addressed to?"

"I don't know. The girls were talking about it in the dining room, but I didn't pay attention."

"What girls?"

"Oh, you know, Edna Brink and them."

Agatha hurried away, thanking Mrs. Teague for the coffee she'd served. This was devastating news. Thaddeus had been a friend of Agatha's almost as long as Lillian. As a grocer, he'd always been industrious and affable. What had driven him to do away with himself? On her way downstairs in the elevator, she pictured Thaddeus's wrinkled face. The lines in the brow looked like worry lines and she wondered if he had gone through life with burdens no one else knew of.

She went down toward the end of the corridor, intending to check with Harriet Hillyard, but when she saw John Beezer's door open and John sitting in a chair bathed in sunlight, she rapped on the door frame and went in.

"Excuse me, Mr. Beezer, I'm told that our friend Thaddeus Druppers took his own life."

John Beezer didn't stand up, but when he saw who his visitor was, he smiled broadly, exposing a mouthful of crooked teeth. He spoke with his eyes averted. "That's right, Missus, gassed hisself in the Mercury. I was the one found him. I was comin' back from the store and I see him settin' there like he's asleep, so I rap on the window, but he's dead as a doornail. I can tell he's dead by the color of his face. It's purple, just like my wife Essie's face when she died in the chair the time the doctor come to the house to tend to Ernie, who was a baby at the time." He pointed to a chair indicating that Agatha should sit.

"Thank you, but I'm just passing by," she told him. "I heard he left a note."

"I heard that too."

"Do you know what it said?"

"No, I never saw it. Sit down and take a load off your feet."

"No, thank you, I'm on my way." She left the room, hearing him call, "Good-bye, Missus."

She found Harriet Hillyard nervous and upset because her son Kirk was to be released from prison. "He'll be out on parole starting next week. Some social worker is supposed to find him a job. Oh, I'm so afraid he'll get right back into the same group of people and break his parole by getting involved again with drugs."

Her clothes—today a well-tailored red pantsuit with a glittery necklace at her throat—made Agatha self-conscious in her plain housedress. "Don't look at me, I've been unpacking," she said. "I came to inquire about Thaddeus Druppers. I was told he killed himself."

"Indeed he did. Carbon monoxide. John Beezer found him and came in and told Mr. Rinkwitz, who called the police."

Agatha was suddenly overtaken by a flood of sorrow. She felt bereft, abandoned first by Lillian and now by Thaddeus. She turned away from Harriet in order to hide her tears. "Why, why?" she said, and her voice broke on the second *why.*

"It must have been guilt over losing the shoebox. He left a note saying he'd lost it."

Agatha gathered herself and turned back to Harriet. "How could he lose it? It must be in the building somewhere?"

"He said it was in Mrs. Kite's coffin."

Agatha was bewildered. A moment passed while she took this in. "Do you mean it's buried in the cemetery?"

"Evidently. He wrote that he had put it in her coffin and then forgotten about it. He said he was very sorry. It's very sad because I don't think anybody had put in really valuable things. He must have been a very conscientious man."

"He was compulsive," said Agatha. She shocked Harriet by chuckling through her tears as she added, "Has anyone suggested digging it up?"

"Edna Brink is making a list of everything in the shoebox before we decide whether to dig it up. She'll be asking you what you put in it."

"I understand he wrote a second postcard to be mailed."

"Yes, I saw that too. It was addressed to your local priest and it criticized him for not genuflecting during Mass. It also said that because he was a suicide, he didn't expect to be buried in the cemetery. Do you understand that, Miss McGee?"

"Oh yes, it goes back to the days when the Church was very strict and unforgiving. Suicide was considered a grievous sin and those who committed it weren't worthy to be buried in consecrated ground."

"Where were they buried?"

"There was a plot outside the cemetery fence, but I don't think anybody was ever buried there. Nobody ever killed himself, as far as I know."

"Until Mr. Druppers. And he was buried inside the fence."

"Yes," said Agatha. "The Church finally came to its senses about suicide. They figure a person has to be out of his mind to take his own life, so he isn't responsible for his actions." She went to the door. "I'd better get back if Big Edna is coming to see me. Please drop by for tea when I get settled. I'm here on the first floor."

"You're not upstairs?"

"No, this time I'm down the hall in 102."

Agatha returned to her apartment in a sorrowful mood, imagining Thaddeus's desperate shame, and dreading the days ahead without the company of Lillian.

Addie Greeno had replaced Lillian as Big Edna's sidekick. They appeared at Agatha's door and demanded to know what she had put into the shoebox.

"Nothing of monetary value, except an old coin," she told them.

"Makes no difference what it was worth," said Big Edna. "We're writing everything down." She strode into Agatha's apartment, displaying a piece of paper, and sat at the kitchen table with her pencil poised.

"All right," said Agatha. "First there was a tile from Assisi, a memento from my trip to Italy in 1986."

"A what?"

"A tile."

"Tile?" asked Big Edna, writing it down.

"Yes."

"What is it?" asked Addie, who stood at Edna's shoulder watching her write.

"Surely you know what a tile is, a flat piece of decorated ceramic material. Mine was small, about four inches square." It was a gift from her soul mate, James O'Hannon, the priest she had toured Italy with. She remembered the day they had stopped in a shop in Assisi and Agatha was immediately taken with the yellow-and-green flower design. She almost bought it herself, but passed it up because she had no use for a tile. Later, as they sat at an outdoor table sipping coffee, dear James had pulled it out of his pocket and given it to her. "Its decoration is a painted flower," she added.

"Value?" asked Big Edna.

"I have no idea. As I say, its value for me is sentimental."

"Well, try to think what you paid for it."

"I didn't pay for it—it was a gift." And then, because Big Edna wasn't giving up but sat staring at her intensely, she said, "Put down five dollars."

Edna wrote it with a triumphant flourish, saying, "What else?"

"A 1902 half dollar. It belonged to my father."

In the value column Edna wrote *.50.* "What else?"

"That's all."

Edna looked crestfallen. "Five dollars and fifty cents won't get the grave dug up. You're the cheapest one so far."

"I don't want the grave dug up."

"You mean you don't want your stuff back?"

"It's safe where it is." She rather liked the thought of her two mementos in Lillian's keeping. There was something fitting about gifts from the two men in her life remaining for eternity with her oldest friend. "Besides," she said. "I know where they are and I won't lose them. Did I tell you I found my diamond brooch? I hadn't lost it after all. It was in my very own closet." She added, "How stupid of me," a gambit that always brought protests from whoever she said it to. But not today. Big Edna and Addie left her with looks of pity on their faces that seemed to say, "You poor stupid dolt."

*   *   *

At two o'clock Agatha went down to the lobby to see who the visiting doctor was, and she found Lillian's daughter, Imogene Kite, sitting on a high stool and reading *The Cat in the Hat* to a small group of women. Puzzled at first, it took her a minute to figure out that the visiting physician was Dr. Seuss.

12

The next day Lillian's daughter Imogene turned up at Friday coffee hour, as did Ernie Beezer and a young man Harriet Hillyard did not introduce but who Agatha assumed was her son Kirk, fresh out of prison. He was a small man with a beard, dressed in an ill-fitting suit. The tie he wore featured the figures of Milne's childhood classic *Winnie-the-Pooh*.

Big Edna passed around the complete list of lost valuables.

Edna Brink
charm bracelet   50.00
china candy dish   25.00
glass & gold earrings   75.00

Addie Greeno
Papal medal   500.00

Harriet Hillyard
billfold   20.00
lottery tickets   00.00

Thaddeus Druppers
shaving brush   00.00
ring   20.00

Agatha McGee

coin	.50
tile	5.00

Lillian Kite

Hankie	2.00
Kleenex, small pack	.50
three earrings	9.00
3/4 roll Tums	.75
cash	2.97
Total	$710.72

Agatha heard Harriet ask Addie Greeno what a papal medal was, but Addie shrugged off the question. She probably didn't remember, but Agatha did. It had been five or six years earlier when Bishop Baker had turned up at Sunday Mass at St. Isidore's to deliver personally to Addie the medal from Rome for her faithful service as priests' housekeeper for thirty-five years. It marked her retirement and it entailed about ten minutes of blessings and prayers. Bishop Baker blessed the medal and then he blessed Addie and finally he blessed the congregation. When Addie returned to her pew, with the medal pinned to her coat, she ignored the applause and continued to wear the same stern expression she wore today in the dining room.

Wasn't Agatha deserving of such an award? Agatha, who had put in forty-seven years as teacher and principal at St. Isidore's Elementary, recalled the surge of jealousy that had come over her as she watched Addie that Sunday morning. This was at a time when Agatha still had a great deal of respect for the pope, the time before he'd lost his voice, his ability to walk and his grip on the Vatican. Worst of all, he hadn't foreseen the looming dangers threatening his Church, those stemming from the short-age of priests. He had refused to consider ordaining women.

Now if Bishop Baker were to present her with a papal medal, she'd have to speak out and bring the hierarchy to its senses.

This was a change of viewpoint for Agatha. It used to be the static quality of the Church that sustained her, its unchangeableness. But now it seemed that the men of the Vatican had not noticed, as she had, the risk of a return to the Dark Ages. She feared that if the Church didn't change with the times and shore up its faltering and diminishing clergy, it would become as obsolete as the Latin Mass.

Big Edna Brink announced that it would cost $800.00 to open a grave and since this list amounted to only $710.72, it wouldn't be cost effective to do so. She asked if there were any objections. Agatha looked at the other depositors. Addie had crossed to another table and was whispering to someone Agatha didn't know, and Harriet was engrossed in something her son was telling her. "Well, I should hope not," screeched Imogene. "If anybody opens my mother's grave, it will be over my dead body. Whose idea was this anyhow?"

"Case closed," said Big Edna.

And so it remained until a few days later, when Harriet Hillyard learned—by telephone from her son Kirk—that she might have put a winning state lottery ticket in the shoebox. Winners were allowed sixty days to come forward and claim the prize, and Kirk said there was a hundred-thousand-dollar jackpot still unclaimed from early December.

After hanging up the phone, Harriet Hillyard went directly to Agatha's door and knocked urgently. "Miss McGee, are you in there?"

It was a sunny morning and Agatha, who had been dozing in her rocking chair, was tempted not to answer, but when the question was repeated and she realized who it was, she crossed through her kitchenette and let Harriet in.

"Miss McGee, I don't know what to do." She repeated her son's message and added, "I threw a number of old lottery tickets into the shoebox, assuming they were worthless. There may have been several from that week because the national jackpot was over a hundred million dollars and I always buy more of everything when it's that high."

"Oh, my goodness," said Agatha, taken aback. She imagined Harriet with a windfall of a hundred thousand dollars and saw in her mind's eye the same well-dressed lady she'd always been. "What would you do with that much money?" she asked.

"Never mind what I'd *do* with it. First I have to *get* it." The poor woman looked distraught. "One minute I tell myself the hell with it, and the next minute I can't stand to think of those tickets six feet underground. I assumed when the week was up, it was a dead issue, forgetting about the sixty-day grace period. Another reason I thought the hell with it is that the tickets are probably worthless, because I've never been lucky that way. I've never won anything in my life—"

"But I thought the jackpot was carried over to the next week. That's how it gets so big. Somebody from West Virginia won over a hundred million dollars before Christmas."

"That's the national lottery. I'm talking about the state lottery." She looked imploringly at Agatha. "It starts fresh with a hundred thousand every two months."

"Well, how would you like me to help you?"

"You're acquainted in town, Miss McGee. If you could talk to the people at the Schwartzman Funeral Home, and tell them my problem, then I could take it from there, arrange for the disinterment and so forth."

Agatha picked up the phone, dialed the funeral home and apprised Linda Schwartzman of Harriet's dilemma. She was told that yes, disinterment could be accomplished with a court order, but it would cost more at this time of year because the ground was frozen solid.

"There's frost to a depth of at least four feet," Agatha told Harriet, "so it will cost eleven hundred dollars. And you'll need a judge's order. And that isn't all—you'll have Imogene to deal with."

"Imogene?"

"Lillian's daughter, Imogene Kite. Lillian used to call her a firecracker."

That afternoon Harriet and Agatha were conveyed to the public library by Little Edna in her tiny, new Honda. They asked her to come in with them, but she declined. Little Edna knew Imogene too well, having hosted her at Friday coffee.

At fifty-seven, Imogene Kite was not aging gracefully. Since her mother's death on Christmas Day, she'd been rather subdued, but she was now coming out of her grief and behaving more like her old self. In Imogene's case, this meant obstreperously. She had obviously exempted herself from the requirement of silence that she imposed on all library patrons. Her voice could be heard throughout the day, not only reprimanding children and adults alike for whispering and returning soiled book covers, but also speaking loudly to herself as she worked.

Standing at the checkout desk, she saw the two women through the glass of the front door climbing the steps. Loudly enough for everyone to hear, she said, "Well, well, if it isn't two old biddies from Sunset."

As they struggled to open the heavy door, Imogene thought how unfair it was that God had taken her mother and left Agatha on earth. Agatha was obviously going to live forever to spite Imogene, who wanted to take her place as Staggerford's matriarch. Never mind that Agatha had outlived that role and that most of Staggerford no longer thought of her as the moral arbiter she had once been; Imogene envied her and wanted to assume the position her mother's friend had once occupied.

Because they entered speaking to each other in low tones, Imogene assumed her sternest look as they approached the desk.

Agatha began, "Imogene, I don't know if you remember meeting Harriet Hillyard at my Christmas dinner or not? Anyhow—"

"Silence," said Imogene. The word rang throughout the reading room, causing the four or five patrons to look up from their papers and books.

Agatha did not lower her voice. "Anyhow, Harriet Hillyard, this is Imogene Kite."

"Yes? I assume she wants a library card."

"No, she wants—"

"Well, it's no use. She has to be a resident six months before I can honor her request."

"Listen, Imogene, get down off your high horse and pay attention," said Agatha, raising her voice. "Mrs. Hillyard has left something quite valuable in your mother's casket and is going to get a court order to dig it up."

Imogene dramatically covered her face and gave out a horrible screech of denial.

"She will explain," said Agatha, stepping away and over to the newspaper rack.

Harriet began to tell Imogene, in a whisper, about her lottery tickets. After a few moments, Agatha was amazed to see Imogene shake hands with Harriet. She was even more amazed to see her smiling benignly down on them as they left the library. "I guess there's no accounting for her change of mood," said Agatha on the front steps.

"Oh yes, there is," said Harriet. "I promised her a cut of my winnings."

Next they crossed the railroad tracks to the law office that used to belong to Agatha's father, where she asked to see Judge Caferty. She and Harriet were asked to sit down and wait for the judge because he was involved in a deposition. Loosening her scarf and opening her coat, Agatha asked Harriet if she had any second thoughts.

"Oh yes, I'm having one now. Those tickets are going to prove worthless, and I'm going to be so embarrassed."

"Well, if you don't want to find out, it will save a lot of people a lot of trouble."

"You yourself wouldn't go through with it, would you, Miss McGee?"

"If I were you . . . I don't know. I don't know how badly you need the money."

"Oh, it isn't for me."

"You're doing it for your son. Kirk has talked you into it."

Harriet answered with a nod and looked away. "You think I'm being foolish," she said to the wall.

Agatha said nothing.

After a minute Harriet turned to face her. "Well, I *am* being foolish—let's go." Both of them stood up to leave, and were buttoning their coats when Judge Caferty opened an inner door and invited them into his office.

"I'm sorry we bothered you," said Agatha. "We were just leaving because we've changed our minds."

"No, we haven't." Harriet shocked Agatha by introducing herself to the judge as she shook his hand and stepped into his office.

As a young man, Maynard Caferty had been a law clerk for Agatha's father. In fact, it was Peter McGee who had set Caferty on his course through law school and then, after he passed the bar (on his second attempt), had taken him into his own office as a practicing attorney. After his career on the bench in Berrington, the county seat, he had reopened his office in Staggerford, where he continued to do some low-profile legal work for old friends.

"Ah, what a pleasure to see you again, Agatha," he said,

taking her hand fondly in both of his own. She remembered him as a nervous young man, but the years—and no doubt the judgeship—had mellowed him, made him expansive like her father, and although she didn't trust him (there were rumors going around concerning bribes and drunkenness), she was always warmed by his greeting.

"Sit down, sit down," he said, pointing to a couch behind a broad coffee table. "Would you like coffee or tea? I could go for a cup of either one."

"Then I'd prefer tea," said Agatha, and Harriet said she'd like the same.

He punched a button on his phone, said the word "Tea," and hung up.

"So, Agatha, you've taken an apartment at Sunset Senior, I'm told."

"Yes, I have."

"And do you have access to a piano, I hope?"

"A piano? No piano, Maynard."

"Oh, what a shame." To Harriet he said, "Agatha used to really like to tickle the ivories."

"I did not. I haven't one speck of musical talent."

"Such modesty. No fibbing now, Agatha. You used to play so sublimely." Again to Harriet: "It was during the war. I used to drop in on the McGees of an evening and Agatha would favor us with something heartrending on the piano. I especially remember 'Don't Get Around Much Anymore.' "

Agatha explained, "I took lessons for four years to please my mother, who was quite musical, until she and my piano teacher finally figured out that I had a tin ear. I was in my thirties during the war and I had long since stopped playing for company."

A young woman whose short skirt, messy blond hair and seductive smile made her look like a floozy to Agatha brought in a teapot and a stack of Styrofoam cups and set them on the coffee table. "Anything else?" she sang to the judge.

"No, that's all," he said, and she left the room.

While he poured, Agatha spoke of the reason for their visit, and she could tell that he was fascinated by Mrs. Hillyard's dilemma. "To dig up a grave we need a court order," she said in conclusion.

"Of course, of course," he said as he picked up his phone. Into it he said, "Give me a letter ordering the disinterment of Mrs. Lillian Kite . . . I have no idea." He asked Agatha, "Two Ls in Lillian?"

"Yes."

He spelled *K-i-t-e* for the secretary and then said, "I think so, just a minute."

He asked, "She's in the Staggerford cemetery?"

Agatha said she was.

"That's right, west of town. Address it to Gil Murphy; he's chairman of the cemetery board. Now get on it."

There was another ten minutes of small talk, during which Agatha had to keep deflecting the judge from the topic of music. Then an older, businesslike woman came in and laid before the judge the letter, which he signed without reading. She said it would go out in the afternoon mail, and the judge said, "I should hope so." The woman hurried away.

Goodness, thought Agatha, the judgeship has made him arrogant as well. She and Harriet stood up and thanked him.

"What's your hurry?" he said. "How about sticking around and we'll have ourselves a real drink." He took a bottle of bourbon out of his desk drawer and mixed himself a drink with the tea. "For old time's sake," he said, holding the bottle out to Agatha and Harriet, but they both turned him down.

Following them through the outer office, where the three secretaries—the older woman, the floozy, and a mousy creature over in a corner—were typing diligently, he said he was going to order a piano for Sunset Senior Apartments and charge it to the state of Minnesota. "Come again, Agatha. Your dad had only one secretary, but otherwise the office is about the same as it was in his day, am I right?"

"The main difference is that my father was never so brusque with his help," she said.

Laughing an embarrassed laugh, Judge Caferty closed the door, said to his secretaries, "She's a real ditz," and went back to his bourbon.

It had begun to snow. At a slower pace than earlier, Harriet went down the street with Agatha, unsure of their next destination. When Agatha opened the door to Schwartzman Funeral and Cremation Services, she stopped. "No, Agatha, not today."

"You're changing your mind again?"

"I'm just needing to sleep on it."

"All right, we'll go to the Hub and meet Little Edna."

The Hub Café, under new management, was closed for remodeling, and the snowfall thickened as they stood outside under scaffolding and waited for Little Edna to pick them up. Harriet said, "Please don't tell anyone about this plan yet. And thank you for all your help. I'm impressed with how you know your way around this town."

"Piffle," said Agatha. "I just happen to know the two people you need to talk to."

"Then there's the undertaker. So that's three."

"Yes, well, Mrs. Schwartzman was my neighbor on River Street. It's pure coincidence."

"And the judge mentioned the chairman of the cemetery board, a man named Murphy. I'll bet you're acquainted with him too."

"Gilbert Murphy," said Agatha, pleased to know four out of four. Maybe she wasn't such a has-been or stranger in town as she'd thought. She smiled at a memory from 1958, the studious and obedient Gilbert Murphy in her sixth grade room, working so hard and systematically on his lessons that Agatha was sure he would end up as an important bureaucrat in St. Paul or Washington, D.C. (Her father, a state legislator, used to bemoan the lack of industrious young people.) But judging from Gilbert Murphy's happy demeanor these days, the fact that he was simply a CPA in Staggerford was apparently a disappointment only to Agatha, not to Gilbert himself or his family.

Little Edna double-parked her Honda while Agatha got into the front seat and Harriet Hillyard got into the back. "Anywhere else you need to go?" she asked them.

"No, thanks, we're finished," said Harriet.

"We're played out," said Agatha, relaxing in the heat of the car. She put her head back against the headrest and was asleep by the time they were back at Sunset.

13

At coffee time on the following Friday, Imogene Kite told everybody at her table about Harriet's dilemma, including Calvin Christianson, the new man living in Lillian's former apartment. Calvin was a tall, pale fellow with a high pile of white hair and bushy white eyebrows, who, like John Beezer, had left a farm to move into the Apartments. His son, like John's, was still farming. His son was married to a terrible fishwife, according to Calvin.

Agatha was so fascinated by Calvin's account of his daughter-in-law's temper that she didn't notice Harriet growing angry beside her as Imogene, across the table, went on and on about the burial of the MX Shoebox and the lottery tickets it contained.

"Some days she'd be as nice as pie, and the next day she'd be a holy terror from morning till night," said Calvin. "I really think it's the weather that did it. It seemed if it was cloudy and overcast, she'd behave just fine; but if the sun was shining, she'd be an out-and-out bitch. Yeah, she was that way from the start. Two years ago when Tom married her and brought her home, she started screamin' at me and the wife about how out of the way our farm was, about the smell of the pigs, about having to do chores every night and morning. The wife tried to settle her down by saying she was right, the farm *was* clear out into the boonies, the pigs *did* smell something awful, and it *was* a bother milkin' seven cows twice a day. Yeah, the wife was pretty much in agreement with her about all that, but it was the girl's screamin' that got to her. Killed her is what it did. See, Lorilee was the unhappiest creature you ever saw and she screamed and complained for two years straight until the wife died and I got the hell outta there. Yeah, I believe it was Lorilee's screamin' that did the wife in."

"Will you please pipe down!" said Harriet across the table to Imogene. She said it in a tone stern enough to hush all conversation in the room, even Calvin's account of his daughter-in-law's unhappiness. "Didn't I ask you to keep this shoebox business under your hat?"

"Well, you've only got about a week left," said Imogene, "and I thought by talking about it—"

"I have until the first of February, that's two weeks from yesterday, thank you very much."

"By talking about it I hoped to get you moving on it, get you off dead center."

"I'll take all the time I need to get moving on it. Just mind your own business!"

"Meanwhile the frost goes deeper and deeper," said Imogene. "If the ground is frozen all the way down, it will take days to dig up my mother."

Harriet Hillyard gave up. She crossed her arms and sat staring at her empty coffee mug, obviously determined to say no more.

Agatha took up her cause, pointing out to Imogene that Harriet had a very good reason for putting off her decision. "She's waiting to see if somebody else comes forward with the winning ticket. If that happens, your mother's body won't need to be exhumed." This was pure speculation on Agatha's part. She assumed it to be true, because Harriet, who had told her nothing about her motives, had let nearly a week pass since their trip to the library and the judge's office.

A long "Ooooooh?" came from the next table—Big Edna's

interest was aroused. "You're going to bring Lillian up after all?" she was asking Agatha.

"Maybe."

"Well, you'll have to do it at your own expense."

"Of course." Agatha turned her attention back to Calvin Christianson, who took up his tale again.

"When he married her and brought her home and we saw what kind of a woman she was, I said to Tom, 'Why don't you take her back where you got her; she's hell on wheels,' but he wouldn't hear of it. Tom's got this loyalty streak, you see. He was the same way with his calf that got sick when he was a boy in 4-H. He had this calf he was groomin' for the county fair that got sick and started wasting away, and I told him, 'Tom, it's no use beatin' a dead horse; better take another one of our calves to the fair.' But no, this was his calf and, dang it, he was determined to show it come hell or high water. Yeah, by the time the fair rolled around his calf was so sick it could hardly stand up, and the vets at the fairgrounds wouldn't let it in the show barn. They was afraid it was hoof-and-mouth, see, afraid of infecting the other animals. Well, it didn't turn out to be hoof-and-mouth because none of my other cattle got it, but we never did find out what it was. Two, three weeks after that we had to shoot the calf."

Later, after coffee, Agatha had two visitors to her room. First came Harriet, in tears because of her tiff with Imogene.

"Buck up," said Agatha, worried now about the mental health of this woman—she'd seen her weeping two or three times in recent weeks. "Imogene's not worth crying over."

Drying her tears, Harriet said she was afraid the disinterment would cost more than she could afford. "I mean if it turns out I don't have the winning ticket. And besides that, I'll look like such a fool."

"Surely your children will help you pay for it," said Agatha.

"No, none of them will kick in a penny."

"You've asked them?"

She nodded and said, "You see, they know it's Kirk's idea and they won't have anything to do with anything he's connected with. He hoodwinked them once too often before he went to prison."

They were interrupted by John Beezer, who stood in the doorway and said, "I want to talk to the new woman."

Agatha stepped forward and said, "Yes?"

"You shook hands with the new man."

"Mr. Christianson. Yes, I did. So?"

"So . . ." John Beezer scratched his head as though confused. "We've never shook hands," he said, stepping forward, his eyes on the floor, extending his hand.

Agatha gave it a brief shake, which seemed to satisfy him. He turned and left.

Harriet Hillyard had to chuckle. "I'd say he has a crush on you, Miss McGee."

"Nonsense," said Agatha. But she wasn't convinced it was nonsense. After Harriet left, she thought more about it and decided the poor man was starved for company and he'd settled on her as a potential companion. But why? She recalled the evening when she'd touched his hand at dinner and asked him where he came from. He'd immediately left the table, Thaddeus said, because she'd invaded his privacy. But maybe he was overcome by a feeling of closeness to Agatha. Maybe that was the beginning of his crush. The next morning he'd brought her the stick of venison.

14

With six days left, Agatha decided that Harriet Hillyard had dillydallied long enough. She knocked on her door rather early in the morning, calling, "No more putting it off, Harriet. I've seen how they dig graves in the winter."

Harriet, who'd been doing her hair, came to the door with a brush in her hand and said, "You mean you think I should go through with it?"

"Yes, of course, you have to, starting today. You see, they burn tires on the surface to thaw out the ground and they dig down a little way with pickaxes, and then they burn the tires over again at the next level. It could take them days to go down six feet. And if money is a problem, I'll pay half."

"Oh, Miss McGee," she squealed, taking Agatha in her arms. "I'll do it."

It was a long hug. When Agatha finally extricated herself, she said, "I didn't realize you were waiting for me to decide." She wanted to warn the woman not to let the opinion of another person dictate her actions, but it felt so good to be in this position that she let it go. She hadn't had the sensation of such power since leaving her job as school principal.

"I haven't been sleeping nights, worrying about whether to go through with it," said Harriet. "I'd just about decide to do it, and then I'd think, what if there's nothing there? I'll look like such a fool."

"There are worse things than looking like a fool and one of them is *being* a fool. You'd be foolish to go through the rest of your life wondering."

"Yes, of course, you're right. I'll just brush my hair and call the funeral home and talk to the mortician."

"You'd better talk to her in person—she'll want a down payment. And I'll go with you," she added. She wanted to be present in case Harriet got cold feet.

On her way back to her room she stopped at the Rinkwitzes' apartment off the lobby to ask for a ride.

The Rinkwitzes, who were having a late breakfast in their kitchen, invited her to join them. She did so, not to eat, but to see farther into their apartment. Their kitchen was much more spacious than the kitchenettes in the other apartments, and like their living room, was hung with every sort of crafty item imaginable. She saw a great number of large wooden cutouts—pheasants, Dutch boys, windmills. Some were unidentifiable. She examined an intricately shaped figure, but was stumped.

"Calvin Christianson makes these," said Little Edna, chewing on a strip of bacon.

"Yes, Calvin's hell on the coping saw," said her husband.

"They're lawn ornaments," Little Edna explained.

Joe said, "But until spring they'll be kitchen ornaments, I'm afraid."

"I shouldn't have to ask," said Agatha, "but what is this one?"

"It's a bluebird," said Edna. "It will look more like it when it's painted."

"He's going to paint it?" said Agatha, dreading the smell of paint and turpentine, which made her wheeze.

She nodded. "All of them—red, white, orange and blue."

"We will vie for the honor of having the most garish front yard in town," said Joe.

Agatha said, "I was wondering if you planned to take your car out today."

"Yes," said Edna, nodding toward her husband. "He's got his Parkinson's support group this morning at ten."

"Because Mrs. Hillyard and I would like a ride downtown."

"No problem. To the library again?"

"No, this time we'd like to go to the funeral home. I realize it's scarcely three blocks away, but this cold weather raises havoc with my breathing."

"So you're going to make arrangements for yourselves," said Little Edna happily.

"No, we just have some business with the undertaker."

Clearing the table, Little Edna wasn't listening. She said, "Preplanning is very wise."

Staggerford's one and only undertaker, Linda Schwartzman, was a large, well-dressed woman who smiled easily. This morning her face was curiously shiny, as if, thought Agatha, she'd left out some crucial stage when doing her makeup. She greeted Agatha effusively and ushered them into her office, a bright, cheery, unmortuarylike room.

Agatha began with the story of the MX Shoebox and explained how it happened to be in the cemetery. Harriet then joined in and told, in a teary voice, about her lottery tickets. She produced from her purse Judge Caferty's letter.

Ms. Schwartzman pondered the letter for a minute as the two women waited uneasily for her judgment. Finally, she looked up, said, "Fine," and dialed her phone. She spoke to someone about opening the grave.

"That was Junior Thompson," she told Agatha and Harriet. "He'll set the first fire today and start digging tomorrow. He says it may take three days to get down to the coffin. Now you understand he doesn't open it. You need some city official or somebody on the cemetery board to do that. Do you have anybody in mind?"

Harriet looked helplessly at Agatha, who said, "Mayor Mulholland. He will surely agree to do that for us."

Ms. Schwartzman dialed the mayor's office and handed the phone to Agatha.

The mayor, who'd never before been asked to open a buried coffin, thought at first that this was a prank call. "Who is this anyhow?" he asked in an irritated voice, then changed his tune when Agatha told him. "Yes, of course I'll do it, Miss McGee. Just call me when it's ready to be opened."

Having made out checks in partial payment, they took their leave of the funeral home, Harriet once again praising Agatha for her command of civic affairs. They walked around the corner to the First National Bank, where Little Edna Rinkwitz would be waiting for her husband, whose support group was meeting in a room the bank provided for them.

"I wouldn't have known where to turn when she told us who should open the coffin, Miss McGee. I had no idea you were acquainted with the mayor."

"He was a student of mine thirty years ago. It's no big deal." But sensing what a big deal it was to Harriet, Agatha was filled with pride and strutted a bit as she entered the bank. She led the way down a flight of stairs, and at the bottom they found themselves in the midst of the support group—twenty or so people, most of them elderly, sipping coffee out of Styrofoam cups as they sat in a circle and listened intently to someone speak in tones too low for Agatha to hear. Little Edna sat next to Joe. When she saw the two women approaching, she got up and opened two folding chairs, placing them on her left and expanding the circle. At first Agatha was amazed to think that twenty people in this area had Parkinson's; then she realized that at least half of them were, like Little Edna, spouses and caregivers. A man sitting opposite her spoke in a slow voice no louder than the one who'd gone before, and she had to listen carefully to what was said:

"I . . . I'm getting to be such a crybaby. I cry, actually break down and cry, over the least little thing. I'll be watching a show on TV and find myself in tears after it's over. I never used to cry. I bet I hadn't cried for forty years before this came on."

"Typical of Parkinson's," said a woman sitting on Agatha's left. She had a mass of dark hair covering most of her face, and she looked younger than the others in the group. Agatha turned and leaned toward her, trying to read the small name tag pinned to her blouse. It said *Sandy Something, Social Worker.* "How many of you others find your emotions coming closer to the surface?" she asked. "Especially crying."

Two or three others raised trembling hands very slowly and timidly, as if thinking it over before committing themselves.

"All right, next is Mrs. Severson."

Mrs. Severson made a couple of starts, but her voice was inaudible, scarcely louder than her breathing, and finally a man sitting next to her explained, "Her voice isn't working today, so I'll speak for her. She falls down all the time. Yesterday she fell in the kitchen and hurt her knee on the tile . . . I guess that's all we have to report. Falling down."

The social worker asked, "How many of you have trouble staying on your feet like Mrs. Severson?"

Three hands were slowly raised, including Joe's, who said, rather proudly, Agatha thought, "I've fallen down three hundred and nine times."

"In how long a time?" asked the social worker.

"Let's see." He considered his answer until Agatha began to squirm impatiently. The others, she noticed, stared at him, unmoving. Finally he said, "Going on three years."

"And have you broken any bones?"

He shook his head. "I seem to be as tough as nails."

"And, finally, Mr. Goosen."

Mr. Goosen's complaint was his loss of dexterity. He said, "I can't screw a screw into the wall anymore, and my handwriting is so small you can hardly read it."

A number of the afflicted nodded slowly, as if they were familiar with this disability, while the social worker said, "Okay, folks, time's up. See you next month." She fled up the stairs.

While waiting for the Rinkwitzes to put on their coats, Agatha was approached by the woman who had fallen in her kitchen. "Miss McGee," she whispered close to her ear. "You don't remember me."

Agatha examined her face and said, "I'm afraid you're right. I don't recognize you."

"I was Margaret Arnold in those days, your student in 1933."

"Margaret Arnold, of course! My goodness, that was sixty-five years ago. You sat in the first row on my right, and you always got a perfect paper in spelling."

"Oh, you remember me." Tears of joy brimmed in her eyes. "This is my husband Myron Severson. Myron, this is the famous Miss McGee."

Shaking her husband's hand, Agatha asked where she'd been all these years. "I'm sure I haven't seen you since the spring of 1934."

Once again her voice failed her and Mr. Severson answered for her. "We farmed north of Willoughby, and we seldom got back to Staggerford. Except now for this group."

They made their way upstairs, Agatha chatting about other students in the sixth grade of 1933–34. Because it had been only her second year of teaching, she remembered it much more clearly than later classes. She knew what had become of a number of Mrs. Severson's classmates because a few had remained in Staggerford and others she'd read about in the obituary section of the weekly paper. When they parted outside the bank, they hugged tightly, and Agatha felt a tremor running through the woman's body.

"An interior kind of shaking that isn't outwardly visible," she called it in the car on the way back to the Apartments.

"I know what you mean," said Little Edna at the wheel. "Joe's got the same thing. It started a couple of years ago and he's been trembling ever since, but not so you can see it."

Little Edna pulled into the circle drive to let her three passengers out at the front door. Joe tripped on his way in, and fell into a snowbank at the side of the walk. "A soft landing," he said, lying prone and smiling. Agatha and Harriet tried to pull him up but weren't strong enough. His wife came around the car and got him on his feet. Her husband thanked her politely and said to the other two women, "Three hundred and ten."

15

At lunch, Big Edna and Addie zeroed in on Agatha, wanting to know all about digging up Lillian.

"What do you mean?" said Agatha, playing dumb. She was conscious of the two men listening at her table, Calvin Christianson and John Beezer.

"Don't be coy," said Addie sternly. "You know what we're talking about."

Agatha came clean: "Of course I do. What I'm getting at is how did you two find out about it?"

"Little Edna mentioned where she took you and Harriet this morning," said Addie. "She thinks it was for preplanning your funerals, but we know better."

"Because of what Lillian's daughter told us at coffee on Friday," added Big Edna. "She said there's a big-money ticket buried with her mother."

"Well, then you know as much about it as I do."

"But we don't know how much," said Addie. "We've heard it's millions, but we don't really believe it's millions."

"Not even close," said Agatha.

They discussed the arduous process of opening a grave in winter, and Addie said she doubted if Junior Thompson was the right man for the job. "He's a sloppy grave digger. His graves were never straight down. Father Finn used to say they went down at an angle."

"He has five days to do it," said Agatha. "That ought to be plenty of time."

"Oh no, he's lazy too," said Addie. "One time Father had a funeral and the grave wasn't ready because Junior Thompson was off on a toot. He was drinking beer down at the pool hall while he was supposed to be digging."

What an irritating creature you are, thought Agatha. *You find fault with everyone who comes up in conversation.* To counteract Addie's bitterness, she said impulsively, "If Junior Thompson bears watching, I'll go out to the cemetery myself and see that he gets the job done right."

Agatha pondered her words through the afternoon and evening and decided it would be a good idea to check up on the grave digger tomorrow, to make sure he got off to a good start. She phoned Frederick and asked if he would take her to the cemetery on his way to work in the morning. He agreed to do it, and thus she found herself sitting on a flat gravestone at sunrise the next morning—a cold, cloudy sunrise—having introduced herself to Junior Thompson, watching him chip away at the hard earth with a pickax. A column of smoke rose into the air from a pile of smoldering tires that lay near the grave. Frederick said he'd return around eleven o'clock, after he sorted his mail and before he began his route, to check on her. The tombstone she sat on belonged to the Pruitt family, father, mother and Miles. Miles Pruitt had been Agatha's lodger and a high school teacher before his life was cut short by Beverly Mulholland's mother. She was deranged and had shot him in the head with a rifle.

Within a half hour Agatha's toes were so cold they ached, and she saw the folly of her plan. When, after an hour, she'd begun to tremble with chills, Junior Thompson, taking a break, came over and offered her coffee from his Thermos. He was a tall man with hair longer than Agatha approved of, but he was friendly and the coffee warmed her. She took a refill eagerly, and when he saw the cup shaking in her hand, he said she ought to climb into his pickup and warm up. "No, thanks, I'm fine," she said, then regretted it as soon as he had gone back to work. *I'm losing my good judgment,* she said to herself. *I'm a fool to be sitting out here in the cold and risking another bout with bronchitis . . .* She was about to tell Junior that she would indeed sit in his pickup, when a rusty, white pickup she didn't recognize pulled into the cemetery and stopped near where she sat. The driver rolled down his window and said, "Hi, Miss McGee, I brought my dad out to check up on you." It was Ernie Beezer.

"Never mind, I'm fine," she said. But to no avail for John Beezer came around the front of the pickup and took in the situation.

"Better get in and warm up," he said, pointing over his shoulder at the rumbling pickup.

She didn't reply but stared at the crusty snow at her feet, afraid to let him see the tears that had started down her cheeks from the cold.

"All right," said John Beezer, as if in response to something she'd said, "I'll take the boy back into town and come out alone. I'll set where you're settin' and maybe then you'll get in and warm yourself up all alone."

"Frederick said he'd come back and pick me up around eleven," she said, but her voice was scarcely more than a whisper and was lost as Ernie gunned the engine and his father got back in. The Beezers drove off in a cloud of exhaust. She saw by her watch that it was nine-thirty.

By the time John Beezer returned, her feet were so cold and numb she could hardly walk and he helped her into the pickup, where it was blessedly warm. She saw that the truck hadn't been cleaned in a long time. The dashboard was dirty and the middle part of the seat where no one sat was covered with grain dust. She drew a hankie from her pocket and dried her cheeks. She saw John go over to the grave and shake hands with Junior

Thompson, who after two hours of work stood only about a foot and a half into the earth. Then he came back and sat on the flat Pruitt gravestone. Her feet and hands gradually became more painful as feeling came back into them. She grew alarmed as the pain worsened, afraid she'd really frozen her feet and perhaps her fingers, so she leaned over and rolled down the driver's window, calling to John Beezer that she'd like to be taken to the emergency room of Mercy Hospital. But John had trudged back to the grave and was consulting with Junior and didn't hear her.

Soon Junior gave his shovel to John, who began to clear away the bits of dirt that Junior loosened with his pickax. After a while they gave up. John, using a long stick, drew the smoldering tires over the grave while Junior carried the ax and the shovel down to the toolshed at the bottom of the cemetery and returned with a can of gasoline. He doused the tires with gas, which caused them to flame up, and a thick stream of acrid black smoke rose into the sky.

"Mighty cold day out," said John, climbing in behind the wheel.

"Terrible," said Agatha. "How did you know I was out here?"

"Heard you talkin' at lunch yesterday. Then this mornin' I see you leavin' with your boy."

"With Frederick," she corrected him. "He's my grand-nephew."

"Oh, he's your grandnephew. Him and Ernie play cards down at the pool hall."

"So your son happened to come to town and you asked him to drive out to the cemetery, is that it?"

"Not hardly. Ernie never comes to town in the morning. No, I called him up and asked him to come in because I had a job to do. I knew if you was settin' out here on a day like this, you'd be colder than a well digger's ass." He chuckled, then glanced at Agatha and stopped chuckling when he saw her look of disapproval. "Well, sir, when I said I had a job to do, he thought I meant we had to haul somethin' somewheres, and so he come in with this here truck, so that's how come you're ridin' in this here pickup instead of his nice new Buick."

"At least it's warm," said Agatha. "That's the main thing."

She was about to ask him to drive to the hospital when she realized that the pain in her toes and fingers had lessened. They rode through town in silence to Sunset Senior, and as he let her out at the front door, the sun came out. Agatha said, "Thank you very kindly, Mr. Beezer."

"No problem. Glad to do it. Tomorrow you stay here where it's nice and warm, and I'll go out and keep tabs on Junior Thompson."

"Oh, I couldn't ask you to do that."

"You ain't askin'—I'm offerin'."

She hurried to her room and took a hot shower. Then she put on her lined slacks and two sweaters and sat in the sunshine, coughing now and then and thinking about John Beezer, and how underneath his crude exterior he was a very generous man.

16

The following evening John Beezer came to supper shivering and needing a shave. He reported to Agatha that Junior Thompson was down almost four feet and tomorrow, with luck, he'd get as far as the coffin.

Big Edna and Addie had questions about the operation, but deferred to Calvin Christianson, who was reminded of a story. "Yeah, I was at a funeral one time where one of the ropes broke under the head end of the coffin as they were lowering it into the grave and the coffin went down headfirst and stayed that way, standing up vertical, you see, and of course nobody wanted to go down there and put it horizontal the way coffins usually go in, and so they covered it up with dirt the way it was, and we all went home. It was old Mrs. Schmittbauer. Yeah, every time she came to mind after that, I imagined her standing on her head in that grave. I suppose if she hadn't been a widow, they'd have straightened her out, but you know how it is when there's no close mourners left alive: it's more of a hurry-up affair. You just want to get it over with. I mean, did you ever notice it's never so sad as when the deceased leaves a spouse or children behind? And not even children, so much as a spouse. That's when it gets sad because you're thinking about the married partner and how he's going to get along without his wife—or husband, as the case may be—and you see him bawling and carrying on, and it gets to you."

John Beezer, bending low over his plate, ate while Calvin spoke. Agatha, sitting to his right, saw him put a large piece of Swiss steak in his mouth and swallow without chewing it properly. He choked on it. Dropping his silverware, he got to his feet and looked desperately around for help. Little Edna, formerly a nurse, came to his aid. She put her arms around him from behind and jerked—the Heimlich maneuver—and the piece of meat went flying across the table and landed on Addie's plate. She stood up, shouting at John, calling him a farmer, a brute and a rapscallion, and left the room. Almost all the other diners remained silent or conversed softly for the rest of the meal.

When John stood up to leave the dining room with everyone else, Agatha asked him to stay. He dropped obediently into his chair but didn't look at her.

"Mr. Beezer," she said, "has that happened to you before? Choking on your food like that?"

"Coupla times," he said, examining his fingers.

"You have to chew properly."

"I know it."

"And while you're at it, I'd like you to chew with your mouth closed. Please."

"Chew with my mouth closed?" He looked at her as though he'd never heard such a crazy idea. "How come?"

"It's the polite way to eat."

"Polite?"

"Yes, polite. You're living in a houseful of women, and some of us are offended by the way you eat."

"You mean Addie Greeno."

"Yes, Addie's one of them. And I am another."

"You?" He seemed not to believe it.

"Me. And another thing, Mr. Beezer, I would like you to sit up straight at the table instead of hunching over your plate with your left hand curled around it."

His face contorted into an expression of anger or sorrow—she couldn't tell which. She stood and looked down at the bald spot at the back of his unruly white hair.

"I'm telling you this for your own good, Mr. Beezer. If you do these two things—sit up straight and chew with your mouth closed—you'll go a long way to being accepted by your house-mates."

She turned to leave the dining room and was surprised to see the Rinkwitzes standing silently behind the serving table. Having listened to her exchange with John Beezer, both of them smiled and gestured their approval—Joe with a thumbs-up and Little Edna with a vigorous nod of her head.

The next day she watched him at lunch. He was better at sitting up straight than he was at chewing with his mouth closed. But he kept making the effort. He kept his mouth closed until it was time to breathe and then he opened it and showed a lot of what he was eating. As for his posture, he'd forget now and then and hunker down over his plate, but as soon as he did, he'd give Agatha a guilty look and straighten up again.

This man wasn't dumb, she told herself. He reminded her of twelve-year-olds she'd had in class who came from deprived backgrounds but were capable of learning as much as she forced upon them. There'd been little Harry Handyside, whose father was trying to raise a bunch of his children by himself while holding down a demanding foreman's job at the pickle factory. Harry had come into the sixth grade as a slovenly urchin who'd been passed through the first five grades without picking up much knowledge along the way. He didn't know his times tables and he read like a third grader. At first he resisted Agatha's strict demands, but she didn't let up. She remembered the day he'd come unprepared to arithmetic class and she'd asked him if he could tie his shoes. Of course he could tie his shoes, he said, and he showed her. Whereupon she stated that anyone who knew how to tie his shoes could easily learn the times tables up through ten. He defied her, apparently determined to be the first shoe-tying student who didn't know eight times seven. So next she lent him a tape player and a tape of her own voice reciting the tables up through twelve. She told him that his homework was to listen to the tape three times a night until he got it all by heart. But this didn't work either. He eventually returned the player, but she never saw the tape again. Finally she appealed to his practical sense, telling him that his father would never have gotten his important job at the pickle factory without knowing his multiplication tables and without knowing how to read. That's all it took. Harry Handyside, aspiring to a job as distinguished as his father's, buckled down and learned his times tables, and by the end of the year he was reading at a ninth-grade level. John Beezer, like Harry Handyside, was educable.

"Will this be the day we open the coffin?" she asked him as they filed out of the dining room. She'd been expecting a phone call from Junior Thompson, who kept a cell phone in his pickup.

"Prob'ly," he said. "I'll drive out and see. Come on along."

"No, thank you, I'll wait for Junior Thompson to call me. And besides, Mrs. Hillyard will want to go out with me."

He went out the back door, where his son was idling a dark-colored Buick. Though the temperature was around zero, he wore no coat or jacket. He got in and they drove away.

Agatha went to Harriet's room and told her the time was near.

"Oh my, the hour of truth," she said. She looked worried. "I should have notified Kirk; he wanted to be here for it."

"I'll go to my room and wait for the call," said Agatha. "I'll also let Mayor Mulholland know."

She found no messages on her phone. Having notified the mayor, she waited for Junior Thompson to call, but he never did. Later, as dusk began to spread across town, John Beezer came to her door and said that Thompson had come upon a big rock and it took him most of the day to dig around it and get the cemetery crane to lift it out.

"My boy Ernie helped him get the rock up and set down beside the grave," he said proudly. "But it was settin' on a slant, and when Thompson got back down in the hole and started diggin' again, the rock slid in and broke his leg pretty bad. Lucky he had a cell telephone in his pickup. Ernie called 911 on it, and an ambulance come and took him into Mercy Hospital."

"Oh, the poor man," said Agatha.

"That boy's dug his last grave for quite some time is my guess."

"I'll call Linda Schwartzman and tell her. She must have a substitute grave digger." She picked up her phone book.

"Otherwise, Ernie and I can finish the job."

"Oh, would you, Mr. Beezer? We'd be so grateful."

"Sure, nothing to it. Thompson was already scrapin' the top of the vault when the rock fell on his leg. We'll start in the morning and be done by noon easy. Ernie'll be down in the hole and I'll be there to help him out. The crane's already there to lift the cover of the vault off."

"Please call me the minute the coffin is ready to open."

"Course, if it snows hard, it'll take longer. The weather report says snow tonight."

"Oh, dear. You know, it's been my policy never to make the weather part of my prayers—I've always let God handle the elements—but tonight I believe the time has come to go against my policy."

John Beezer turned away, chuckling and shaking his head.

"What is it, Mr. Beezer? What are you laughing at?"

"Leavin' God to take care of the elements. I don't know— you take the cake, Missus." Then hurrying to change the subject, he looked at his watch. "Five minutes till supper," he said. "Should we go together?"

"You run along. I'll call the mayor and let him know what happened."

By the time she reached her table, the dining room chatter was about what most of the residents had just seen on the five o'clock news—pictures of John Beezer himself, standing in the cemetery being interviewed.

"Why *him,* of all people. He can't even talk right."

"It was all about Lillian's grave being dug up."

"They should interview Harriet Hillyard—it's her lottery ticket they're looking for."

"Boy oh boy, that place will be a zoo tomorrow."

"You're right. Everybody and his brother will be out there to see the casket come up. If I had a car, I'd go myself."

"Say, Rinkwitzes, how about a ride out to the cemetery tomorrow?"

John Beezer glanced at Agatha, but evidently didn't see her look of fierce disapproval as the talk swirled around her, for he straightened up and looked very proud of having appeared on television.

After the meal, Agatha accompanied him down the hallway. She was on her way to check on Harriet, who had missed supper. "It's a great disappointment to me that the news got out, Mr. Beezer. This is a private affair, not for television news coverage."

"Yeah, that's what I told that Larem woman."

"You told whom?"

"Jessica Larem. She's on at five ever' day."

"But you allowed her to interview you."

"Naw. She just asked me a few questions."

"And you answered them."

"Sure, the ones I knew the answers to."

"That's what you call an interview."

He said, "Naw," and then he said, "Is that right? Well, I be danged. I always thought a interview was where you could see a long ways across the land."

Harriet stepped out of her apartment and stood listening.

"No, you're probably thinking of a panoramic view."

"Panoramic? No . . ." He searched his mind for a moment. "No, I never heard of paramatic."

"Well, never mind. Tomorrow, if there are reporters in the cemetery, we'll ignore them."

"Did I ever tell you my wife's sister was her aunt by marriage?"

"Whose aunt by marriage?"

"Jessica Larem. She was niece to my wife's sister Clara before she died. She come to the funeral."

Agatha turned to Harriet. "You weren't at supper."

"I turned on the news and saw all about the grave digger and I was too embarrassed."

"So you know about the delay. Mr. Beezer here is going to finish the job for us tomorrow, he and his son."

John Beezer said, "See, the wife's sister's husband was uncle to Jessica Larem, and she married him and then she was her aunt."

"Tomorrow there may be a lot of reporters at the cemetery," Agatha repeated to John, for Harriet's benefit. "We'll go about our business and ignore them."

Harriet asked timidly, "I suppose I'll have to be there?"

"Well, of course," said Agatha, perturbed at her new friend for losing heart. "Mr. Beezer will call me and I'll call you and Mayor Mulholland. The mayor will pick us up and drive us out there. He'll open the coffin and hand the shoebox to Big Edna, who insists it's her job to open it, since she was its self-appointed caretaker. She will take out what you put in and you will read the numbers on the tickets. While you're doing that, Mr. Beezer and his son will begin filling in the grave."

"And what time do you expect this will happen?"

"Mr. Beezer thinks around noon."

"Unless we get dumped on by a pile of snow," he said. "Then it'll be more like three or four."

"We intend to pray for no snow tonight," said Agatha, turning to go back to her room.

John Beezer followed her down the hallway, saying, "The wife's sister didn't stay married to him very long, though. He was a no-good guy. Never could hold a job. Spent all her money. That whole Larem family was teched, if you ask me. Except Jessica herself. She's a straight shooter. Not lazy in the least. You can tell that by talkin' to her."

Agatha bade him good night at her door, which she locked behind her.

Later, getting into bed, she turned off her light and saw snow piling up outside her window. She immediately went to work with her rosary. But her prayers were no match for the snowfall, which she watched until midnight, coming down in sheets.

17

The next morning, Agatha woke to a changed world. Two feet of snow covered everything. The cars parked behind her apartment were unrecognizable white mounds and the alleyway was impassable. A mammoth beer truck was stuck behind the liquor store and it took three men an hour to dig it out. Around ten o'clock the sun appeared and a breeze came along to blow the snowcap off the bird feeder. Near noon a plow came down the alley, creating a high snowbank in the yard behind Sunset Senior, and Staggerford began to function again.

At one o'clock John Beezer called to say they'd been delayed by the snowfall. Getting stuck three times, it took them forever to get to the cemetery, and when they got there, they discovered the grave filled with drifting snow, which Ernie was now about finished shoveling out. John thought they'd be ready for sure in an hour's time.

Agatha phoned Mayor Mulholland and Harriet Hillyard. She debated with herself about calling Big Edna, and finally did so in order to avoid recriminations. Soon Agatha and Big Edna were waiting in the lobby for the mayor's car, and in a few minutes they were joined by Harriet, and—to their surprise—Kirk Hillyard.

"Miss McGee, this is my son Kirk," she said quickly and with a nervous quaver in her voice. "Kirk, this is Miss McGee. I've told you what a great help she's been. Why if it hadn't been for her—"

"Pleased t'meetcha," said Kirk, giving her a handshake so firm it hurt. He wore a leather jacket, had a pock-marked face and his mouth was crimped in a small perpetual smile. Agatha thought him quite sinister looking and her heart went out to Harriet. She wanted to tell her that she could see why her son upset her so.

"And this is Edna Brink," said Harriet. "She's in charge of the shoebox."

"Nice t'meetcha," he said, hurting Big Edna's hand as well.

Agatha softened toward Kirk momentarily when she thought he was opening the mayor's front passenger door for her, but then he got in himself. The three women let themselves in the back. Agatha pulled the door shut as Mayor Mulholland and Kirk were introducing themselves, and she could tell by the sudden scowl on the mayor's face that Kirk was giving him a painful handshake.

The cemetery was a mile west of town. It was an uncomfortable ride, as Agatha and Harriet were squeezed on either side of Big Edna. The mayor was telling Kirk that he'd never done this sort of thing before, opened a coffin, and it gave him the willies to think about it.

"We'll make it worth your while," said Kirk. "We'll give you twenty dollars."

At this Mayor Mulholland fell silent, offended, Agatha supposed, by the offer of money for a duty that went with his job.

A sudden roaring sound caused them to crane their necks and look up to see a helicopter. "A news crew!" said Kirk excitedly, seeing the bright red letters KSTP blazoned on its side. The helicopter hovered over the cemetery, then, after kicking up a cloud of snow, it rose again but didn't go away.

They were relieved to see that the cemetery lanes had been

plowed but were surprised to see six or eight vehicles lined up along the main lane. Agatha thought they represented a funeral in progress until Kirk said, "Hey, more reporters," and read aloud, as they passed, the call letters off the sides of the vans and cars. "WCCO, KFGO, KRKU. Fargo, Minneapolis and Rookery are here!" he added triumphantly.

"We will ignore them all," Agatha directed as Mayor Mulholland parked as close to Lillian's grave as possible. It was very cold. The sky was clear and the sunshine on the snow was blinding. They followed a slippery path of packed snow across several graves, the mayor taking Agatha's arm and leading the way. Agatha saw John Beezer point in her direction and several cameramen turned and aimed their Minicams at her. Reporters rushed over to her, with microphones and tape recorders at the ready.

"Miss McGee, how much money is the lottery ticket worth?" was the main question they all put to her. To each of their inquiries she answered, "No comment," through the scarf she held over her mouth to make breathing easier. The reporter from KRKU Rookery, a balding young man with no cap on his head who, having spent the sixth grade at St. Isadore's, knew Agatha, took her other arm and walked side by side with her and the mayor toward a camera, spilling his newscaster's lingo into a microphone as they went:

"I have here Miss Agatha McGee, who used to be a regular call-in guest of Lolly Edwards's, who many of you will remember used to broadcast her program, *Lolly Speaking*, from our studios in Rookery. Miss McGee, who once upon a time was a schoolteacher in Staggerford, is the most respected old person in Berrington County and so we are all very eager to hear her take on what's going on today in the Staggerford cemetery." They came to a stop at the graveside, where Ernie Beezer, standing at a small crane, was lifting the cover of the concrete vault up to ground level. "So, Miss McGee, what do you have to say about all this?" asked the reporter, thrusting his microphone in her face.

"I have to say that if you don't wear something on your head, you're going to get pneumonia. It's below zero."

Her acerbic tone apparently scared off the other newspeople. They began to pick on the others and left Agatha alone. She heard Big Edna say, "It's called the MX Shoebox," and Kirk Hillyard explained that the lottery ticket was worth a hundred thousand dollars.

With the vault opened, it was Mayor Mulholland's job to descend into the grave and open the coffin. Agatha was glad that dirt banks and snowbanks were piled around the grave and kept her from standing at the edge and looking in. She saw the mayor disappear into the grave and a minute later hand the shoebox up to John Beezer, who happened to be standing closest.

"I'll take that," said Big Edna, snatching it out of his hands and striding toward the car with Kirk Hillyard and the news crews following close behind. Agatha and Harriet clung to each other as they brought up the rear. The pitch of the reporters' questions rose as they watched the shoebox disappear inside the car. This time Kirk, in his eagerness to get at the tickets, got into the backseat with Big Edna and his mother, leaving the front seat for Agatha. They locked the doors and waited for Mayor Mulholland, who had stayed behind to help the Beezers lower the cover of the vault.

"Well, come on, aren't you going to open it?" said Kirk. "I remember the first three numbers of the winning ticket—thirty, twenty-eight and seven. I forget what comes next."

Big Edna drew from her coat pocket a small, serrated kitchen knife wrapped in a paper towel. She sawed through the packing tape around the cover and lifted it off. Agatha turned and faced front, not wishing to see Kirk practically drooling with avarice. "Here's the billfold," she heard Big Edna say. She had evidently handed it to Harriet because Kirk whined, "Hey, give it here."

Harriet said, "Here they are, two state tickets." Agatha braced herself for cheering from the backseat but heard nothing but a long silence. Then Kirk said, under his breath, "Dammit, dammit, Goddammit." He repeated this several times until Mayor Mulholland, getting in behind the wheel, glared at him.

"Well, what am I supposed to do for money?" said Kirk.

"Do what most other people do," said Agatha. "Get a job!"

"Get a job! I can't get a job; I'm an ex-con."

"Or go on welfare," added the mayor.

The next night on TV, Agatha saw a news item about a certain Mr. Albert Johnson of Berrington, a haggard-looking man in a denim jacket, who had come forward at the last minute with the winning lottery ticket. Asked why he'd waited so long, he said, "I got a whole bunch of relations who'll try to get their hands on this money, and me and my lawyer took quite a little while to figure out how to keep it to myself."

"And what will you do with all this money, Mr. Johnson?"

"Quit my job, first thing. I work at the canning factory in Berrington. They can take that job and shove it."

18

Opening Lillian's grave was much on Agatha's mind the next day. The more she thought about it, the more she was struck by the generosity of John Beezer and his son. They had spent the entire day out in the five-below temperature and asked nothing in return. She wrote John Beezer a note, thanking him and Ernie for their help. She sealed the envelope and was about to put a stamp on it, but then thought better of spending thirty-three cents when she could hand it to him personally.

She realized, too, that despite not finding the winning ticket, the project had energized her. This was due mainly to the respect she got from Harriet Hillyard. Having fed on the high regard that Staggerford had bestowed on her all her life, she'd been starving for it the last few years, and particularly the last few weeks since moving into her Sunset Senior apartment. Knowing only four of the other residents, she'd been feeling marginalized and useless. She'd spent many of her meals in the dining room simply eating, without taking part in conversations. She was seldom asked her opinion of anything, and if she had been asked, she probably wouldn't have had one because half the time she didn't understand what her fellow residents were talking about. Many of them came from farms and discussed the price of milk and hay and eggs. The others were forever talking about their bridge games, but Agatha had never learned to play bridge. In fact, she hadn't played a hand of cards of any type since Miles Pruitt had died more than a quarter of a century ago. She and Miles used to get out the cribbage board now and then . . . *Fifteen two, four, six, and a pair is eight.* She thought about Miles and the injustice of his early death. She'd never known anyone quite like him. Troubles rolled off him like water off a duck's back. He was so soft-spoken and easygoing you'd be tempted to say that he was indifferent toward life, but when you got to know him, you discovered he cared very deeply about people. Agatha remembered how he used to agonize over his students' papers. She could still picture him sitting at the dining room table with his briefcase open beside him and groaning as he read. When it came to grading, he was concerned that a D or F might discourage a student, so he always graded, in Agatha's opinion, too high. More than once she'd advised him to grade the way she did—four grammatical errors or misspellings earned the student an F, three meant a D, two a C, one a B, and none an A—but he was stubborn as a mule. Invariably, he'd thank her very kindly for her advice, then, mumbling something about his fear of stifling an ego, he'd go ahead and give his student too much credit.

In giving the thank-you card to John Beezer at supper, she'd underestimated its powerful effect. He tore it open, read the brief message and proudly handed it around the table for everyone to see. Addie, when it came her turn, looked from John to Agatha in disbelief, as if to say, you're asking for trouble with that crazy man. She said as much to Agatha on their way out of the dining room.

"You're getting much too friendly with that boor, Agatha. A word to the wise—he's a nutcase, and you'll be sorry."

"I'll thank you not to dictate who my friends should be, Addie."

John Beezer, walking directly in front of them, heard this exchange, and he paused to let them go by and then followed

Agatha to her room. As she unlocked her door, he said, "You sure do take the cake, Missus."

"You've told me that before, Mr. Beezer. What does *taking the cake* mean, exactly?"

He thought about it. "Well, it means you're quite a woman, is what it means."

"And what do you mean, I'm 'quite a woman'?" She let her door swing open but remained in the corridor.

"Besides having a lot of spunk, you know your manners."

"That's not so unusual, Mr. Beezer. Most of our companions here know their manners. And as for spunk, I had spunk once, but what you're seeing now, I'm afraid, is only a shadow of my former self."

"No, you've still got it. I heard you put that Greeno woman in her place just now, and I saw how you sat at the cemetery all that one morning."

"Well, yes, Addie Greeno requires a reprimand now and again. But as for the cemetery, that was very foolish of me. I'm afraid I'm coming down with a cold."

"I got some yellow pills that take care of colds overnight. Come down to my room; I'll give you some."

"Never mind," she said. "I can go across to Kmart in the morning."

"Morning's too late; you gotta catch it early. Come on."

He started down the hallway. She locked her door and followed him.

In his living room she was surprised to find Ernie Beezer visiting with Kirk Hillyard. Kirk occupied the only easy chair, with his knee up to his chest and his foot bare. He was trimming his toenails with a nail clipper and dropping the clippings on the carpet. He paused to glance up at Agatha but said nothing. Ernie sat facing him on a straight chair and said, "Hi, Missus McGee."

"How do you do, Mr. Beezer. I think the time has come to

straighten out you and your father concerning my name. It's Miss McGee, not Missus McGee."

He called to his father, who had stepped into the bathroom, "You hear that, Dad? She's a miss, not a missus."

"Yep," said John, emerging with a small bottle of antihistamine tablets. "Here, Missus, these'll do the trick. Take two right away and one every four hours tomorrow and your cold'll be history." He spilled half a dozen tablets into her hand.

She thanked him and said good-bye. Ernie said, "See you later," but Kirk said nothing. John followed her out into the hallway, explaining, "Them two are plotting to kidnap Ernie's girl."

This stopped Agatha in her tracks. She said, "Kidnap whom?"

"Jennie. Ernie's girl. She's four years old. No, maybe she's five; I forget. See, Ernie used to be married to this awful woman named Beatrice. She lives in Bartlett with their daughter Jennie, but she won't let Ernie see her. So they're going to take her away."

"Mr. Beezer, that's a serious crime. I hope you're going to stop them."

"Stop 'em? Why should I stop 'em? Ernie's got a right to see his own daughter. It's written down in the divorce settlement. He's s'posed to have her ever' other weekend."

"Mr. Beezer, if you don't stop them, I will."

"You?" His face fell. He looked pitifully disappointed. "But I thought we were . . . friends."

"Friendship doesn't allow for a crime to take place. I will have to call the police." She crossed the hall to Harriet's door and knocked.

"Don't call the police, Missus," he said desperately to her back. "Please don't call the police."

"You stop them and I won't," she said.

Harriet looked fretful but seemed happy to see Agatha. Letting her in, she looked across into John Beezer's apartment to see if Kirk was still there. She invited her guest to sit in one of two easy chairs facing the television.

"I haven't told you how sorry I am about the lottery ticket," Agatha said as she settled in the soft chair and Harriet turned down the television's sound but left the set on.

"Thank you, Miss McGee, and I'm sorry for all the trouble you went to."

Agatha dismissed the woman's thanks with a wave of her hand. "Two trips downtown and two trips to the cemetery were no trouble. I just stopped by to check on you, since you weren't at supper again tonight. You look a little under the weather."

"Oh, you're too kind, Miss McGee. I'm fine. Or I should say I will be fine when my son is on his way. You see, he stayed here last night. He slept on the couch and we ate together. That's why I haven't been to the dining room."

After being momentarily distracted by a picture of five women in ball gowns on television, Agatha asked, "How long does he plan to stay?"

"Not long. Just tonight. John Beezer's son offered him a job and he jumped at the chance."

"What sort of a job?"

"They didn't tell me, but the money is good. I assume it's farm work. All Kirk needs is money to get started in life."

One of the young women in ball gowns stepped forward and spoke with the emcee. MISS DELAWARE was flashed on the screen.

Agatha was about to tell her friend what Kirk and Ernie were planning across the hall when she heard a shout and the sound of a scuffle. Harriet heard it too, and went to her door. Opening it, she saw her son in John Beezer's doorway. He was getting up off the floor with a bloody nose. Stepping up behind her, Agatha saw Ernie Beezer opening and closing his fist, flexing it and then massaging it with his other hand. Glancing up, Ernie saw Harriet and said, "Sorry, Mrs. Hillyard, but Kirk just went for my dad. I can't stand for anybody laying a hand on my dad."

"Whatever for?" said Harriet. "Kirk, why did you go after Mr. Beezer?"

Kirk didn't answer. He went back to the easy chair and sat down.

"How is your father?" asked Agatha.

"He's fine," said Ernie. "Kirk never got to him."

John Beezer verified this by appearing in his doorway and saying, "I'm fine. Ernie here stopped him before he got to me."

Ernie said to the women, "See you later," and shut the door.

"Why in the world?" said Harriet. "I've never known Kirk to go after people."

"I think I know the reason," said Agatha. "Those two young men are hatching a plan to kidnap Ernie's daughter and John probably said he was going to stop them." She explained what John had told her about his daughter-in-law.

"Oh, Agatha, I'm not used to people with such troubles. I don't know if I can stay here."

"Of course you can stay," Agatha told her. Desperate to keep her as a friend, Agatha didn't point out that it was Harriet's son who was the troublemaker. "Just speak to Kirk and stop him from taking part in the crime, and everything will be all right."

Harriet turned up the television sound and the two of them watched the rest of the beauty contest over tea.

19

The next day, midafternoon, Agatha answered a pounding on her door and found Kirk Hillyard standing there with a little blond girl about five years old. She wore a pink dress and a jacket many sizes too big for her. "Here," said Kirk, "You take her till her daddy comes for her." He took the jacket from her shoulders—it was his—and hurried away, with Agatha and the girl looking after him. They saw him turn and go out through the main entrance rather than continue down the corridor to his mother's room.

I'll call the police immediately, Agatha told herself; *I won't be arrested as part of this hellish plot.* But looking down at the girl, she saw that her face was streaked with tears and her nose was running. She took her into her apartment and shut the door, leading her to the bathroom for Kleenex. Dabbing at her cheeks, she asked what her name was. The girl evidently found Agatha's timeworn face frightening because as soon as she looked up at it, saying "Jennie," she burst into renewed tears.

"Now don't cry; we'll call your grandpa." Agatha led her by the hand back into her living room and dialed John Beezer's number. No answer. She dialed Harriet's number. Again no answer. She was about to dial 911 and ask for the police when Jennie, through her tears, asked Agatha if she had any cookies.

"Goodness, child, are you hungry? Well, you just come with me."

They moved into the kitchenette and sat at the table. With Jennie munching on a Hydrox, Agatha asked if she went to school.

The girl answered weakly, "Kindygarden."

"I see, and what school do you go to?"

"The one by the post office."

"In Bartlett?"

After a moment's thought, the girl nodded.

"Do you know a Miss Hillyard? She teaches there."

Jennie finished the cookie and whimpered softly.

"I know exactly what you're feeling," Agatha told her. "Two months ago when I first moved in here, I wanted to cry myself."

The thought of this old lady weeping obviously amused the girl for she smiled a little through her tears.

"Oh yes, I sat in that rocking chair over there and one afternoon I may have actually shed a few tears. Life is so short, but the afternoons are so long, don't you agree?" She moved the cookie plate closer to the child. "Displacement is a terrible thing. That's what you're feeling right now, displaced."

Jennie took a second cookie and asked, "Can I have some milk?"

Luckily, Agatha, who liked milk in her tea, had recently bought a quart. She poured a glass, which the girl took and drank thirstily.

"You see, I also thought that somebody had stolen my best piece of jewelry, and that made me doubly sad. But it hadn't been stolen after all. I had simply misplaced it, and after accusing a number of people of taking it, I found it pinned to a blouse in my closet."

Jennie seemed fascinated by this story. She stopped eating and drinking and stared at Agatha. Her eyes, which were dark blue, almost black in fact, were so penetrating that Agatha grew uncomfortable.

She said, "Would you like to see my jewelry?"

Cheered by the invitation, the girl nodded as she stuffed the rest of the cookie into her mouth. Agatha wet a fresh dishrag at the sink and wiped up the crumbs, wiped Jennie's face and fingers. She then led her into the bedroom, where she opened a drawer of her dresser and lifted out her jewel box.

Jennie wasn't as interested in the diamond brooch as Agatha had expected her to be. Her favorite piece was a pink coral necklace. She asked Agatha to put it on, which she did. The girl studied it for a moment, then took it back and draped it around her own neck. She went over to Agatha's dressing table and admired herself in the mirror. "This is good," she said, and went into the living room and sat down in front of the television. She said, "Mister Rogers is on."

"Oh, we don't watch TV during the daytime," said Agatha, whose attitude toward television could be described as distrustful. She had learned as a teacher how it could make children, as well as some adults, TV-dependent slaves.

The girl stared at her in disbelief.

"We only watch it in the evening sometimes," she explained. "For the news."

The girl wept and screamed so loud that Agatha quickly switched on the television and found Mister Rogers putting on his slippers.

They sat side by side watching, Jennie sucking her thumb and fingering the coral necklace with her other hand, Agatha engrossed in the show. She loved Mister Rogers instantly, particularly his polite, soft-spoken manner with children. When the show ended, she asked Jennie if it was on every day.

No answer. The girl was asleep.

Jennie slept until dark and woke to find Agatha working quietly at her stove, heating a saucepan of Kraft macaroni and cheese. This had been a staple of Agatha's diet when she was teaching—she had never been interested in mastering the culinary arts—and she was given to understand that little children liked it too. When she saw Jennie awake, she went to her phone, intending to call the police, but decided to dial Harriet's number instead. Again there was no answer. Agatha looked at her watch and took this to mean that Kirk was still gone and Harriet was already in the dining room for supper.

Next she dialed John Beezer's number and was surprised when a voice said, "Ernie here."

"Oh, Mr. Beezer, is your father there?"

"Nope, who wants to know?"

"This is Agatha McGee, and I have your daughter here."

"You got Jennie? What apartment you in?"

"I'm in 102, but please give us half an hour. We are about to sit down to supper."

Ernie slammed down the phone before she finished speaking, and within a minute he came knocking on her door. As soon as she opened it, Jennie shouted, "Daddy," and came running. He gathered her up in his arms.

"How did you get here?" he asked her.

"Young Mr. Hillyard brought her," Agatha explained. "Around three or so."

"So where is he?"

"I have no idea. He left the building right away."

"That sumbitch stole my car."

"You weren't in when he came. That's probably why he left her with me."

Jennie was giving Agatha a superior look now that she was secure in her father's arms. Agatha patted her on the knee and she buried her face in her father's neck.

"That sumbitch stole my Buick."

"Yes, so you've said."

"He wasn't s'posed to bring her till suppertime. Where did he pick you up, Jennie?"

"He came to school."

"I give the sumbitch my car keys and a wad of money around three o'clock and told him to pick up Jennie at her sitter's house at five-thirty." He lowered his daughter to the floor. "Stay here with the nice lady. You can go down to Grandpa's room when he gets done eating. I'm going to find that sumbitch with my car." He asked Agatha, "Do you have a car I can borrow?"

"I have no car."

"Damn." He started down the hall, and his daughter started after him. Agatha hurriedly pulled her door shut and followed. Jennie screamed when she took her hand. Agatha let go and walked beside her, following Ernie into the dining room.

"Has anybody got a car I can borrow for half an hour?" he asked the residents in a booming voice. His father, evidently puzzled, turned in his chair to look at him. Many others turned to stare at Agatha, as if she had no business in the dining room.

Calvin Christianson asked, "Where do you need to go?"

"Bartlett."

"Wait a minute and I'll take you to Bartlett."

"I can't wait," said Ernie. "Anybody else?"

John Beezer made beckoning gestures to Jennie, but she clung to her father's pants leg.

Because there were no other offers, Ernie told Calvin that he'd be waiting at the door to the back parking lot, and he swept out of the room with Jennie at his heels and Agatha following.

At the back door, looking out at the six or eight cars parked in the snow, she asked Ernie how he knew Kirk was in Bartlett.

"I don't know; I'm guessing," said Ernie, picking up his daughter again. "He has a sister there."

"But what if he's not there and Mr. Christianson won't take you beyond Bartlett?"

"He won't need to. I'll just have him take me to the farm and I'll get my pickup."

Agatha said, "Mr. Beezer, you're committing a high crime, a kidnapping. I refuse to be involved further."

"Listen, it's my ex-wife who's the criminal. Our custody agreement has me seeing Jennie every other weekend. Do you know how long it's been since Jennie and I were together?"

"Two wrongs don't make a right, Mr. Beezer."

"It's been six weeks. So now if Beatrice sends the law after me, I've got that on my side—Beatrice never abided by the agreement. I give Kirk two hundred dollars to pick her up at the sitter's the minute she stepped out the door to walk home at five o'clock. The sitter's house is practically on the same block as Beatrice's. She works at the turkey processing plant as a book-keeper, and she gets off work at quarter to five. Well, what that sumbitch did was went and got her out of school, which I told him specific not to do because the sitter picks her up after school and she'd recognize my Buick. So what he musta did, he musta went in and got her out of class before school let out."

He asked Jennie, "Did the man come get you before school was out?"

Instead of answering, she said she was hungry and began whimpering.

"So that's what he musta did," said Ernie. "And then he took off with my car. Well, I'll take care of that sumbitch."

Calvin Christianson came out of the dining room jingling his car keys and said he was going to his apartment for a coat and he'd be right back.

"Okay, Jennie, I'll be back," said Ernie, setting her down on her feet. She raised her whimper to an ear-piercing scream and when he picked her up she beat him on his chest with her fists. He carried her back to Agatha's door, saying, "Possession is nine tenths of the law, I've heard it said. Jennie's in my possession now and they'll never get her back."

Agatha acquiesced. There was nowhere else to leave the girl—everyone was still at supper. She dreaded having this confused child in her apartment screaming, but Jennie quieted down as soon as her father left and *The Price Is Right* appeared on TV. Agatha dished up the macaroni, and they ate in front of the television set. When the program ended, the girl turned to Agatha and asked, "What's on next?"

"I have no idea. I suggest we play a hand of cards." Agatha went to the kitchen drawer where she kept her cribbage board and an old deck of cards held together with a rubber band.

"What day is it?" asked Jennie.

"It's Thursday."

"Thursday?" Jennie brightened. "Then *Law & Order* is on channel nine."

Agatha set a TV table between them and put down the cribbage board and pack of cards, but Jennie was interested only in *Law & Order*, which they watched in its entirety, Agatha gasping at three grisly murders and a corrupt city official, Jennie taking it all in without comment or reaction of any kind. After it was over, Jennie agreed to turn off the television in exchange for a cup of cocoa and more cookies. Then Agatha made up a bed for her on her love seat and the girl immediately fell asleep.

Expecting Ernie Beezer's return any minute, Agatha stayed up until nearly midnight, watching Jennie sleep and trying to figure out why she had not called the police. It had something to do with the girl herself. Jennie called up in Agatha an emotion like the one she used to feel in her teaching days, an attachment she felt for all her students, particularly the down-and-outers, those who came from deprived circumstances. It was an intellectual kind of maternal instinct, a groping for a meeting of minds. This poor television-addicted child needed a good bit of training, needed to be talked out of screaming every time she didn't get her own way.

But was this any reason not to call the authorities? Surely this was a crime worthy of police intervention. Never mind if the divorce agreement had been violated, this child had been taken from her mother. She must call the police first thing in the morning. And if not the police, then Mayor Mulholland. Yes, that would be much easier. She would leave it in the mayor's hands.

20

Agatha was awakened at 7:15 A.M. by the sound of TV—Jennie watching cartoons. She straightened her hair in the mirror, and with her bathrobe held tight to her throat she went out into the living room and asked Jennie if she'd said her morning prayers. The child didn't seem to understand, didn't take her eyes from the screen, her solemn attention held by a funny-looking animal shooting a gun at a funny-looking man. Agatha gave up. Later she took her cordless phone into the bedroom and dialed the Mulhollands' house, hoping to catch the mayor before he left for the office. She got Beverly Mulholland instead, who said her husband had already left, but would call her as soon as he came home for his midmorning break.

Having prepared herself for revealing all, Agatha was disappointed and frustrated. She needed to tell somebody, so she dialed her friend Janet Meers's number in Florida. Janet and her husband, Randy Meers, a Realtor, had been wintering in Vero Beach since before Thanksgiving. Randy had bought four houses in a gated community near the ocean, one for himself and three as income property.

"Janet, remember when I told you about the big lie I told? The one about the Holister sisters in Willoughby?"

"Sure, you said the wrong sister died, and you got away with it. Everybody still thinks Calista Holister is her sister."

"I also said it was the first serious sin of my life, remember?"

"Agatha, stop worrying about it. You did it for a noble reason. It's water under the bridge."

"Well, be that as it may, I'm calling to say that I'm now involved in a much more serious sin."

"I have a potential renter here who wants to look at our house next door. Can I call you back?"

"This won't take long. I'm involved in a kidnapping."

Janet shrieked, "What?"

Agatha explained.

Janet's first reaction was to blame the mother. "She's probably no good, Agatha, and after all, she broke the divorce agreement." Because this didn't seem to mollify her, Janet added that Agatha was innocent because she had done nothing to promote the kidnapping. "You happened to be home when the man dropped her off. You can't blame yourself for that."

"No, you're right about that, but my sin is concealing what I know from the authorities. That makes me a conspirator, a henchwoman."

"Never mind that, Agatha. What do you know about the girl's mother?"

"Only that she lives in Bartlett and she's a secretary or bookkeeper at some firm there."

"Well, if I were you, I'd want to find out what her mother's like before I'd turn her father over to the police."

"No, you miss the point, Janet. I—"

"I'm sorry, Agatha, I have to run; I'll call you back."

Talking to Janet never helped matters anyway, Agatha thought, because Janet always came down on her side, no matter what the issue—which was all very encouraging, of course, but this morning Agatha needed somebody who wasn't weak on the topic of morality. She dialed the rectory and got Father Healy's voice on his answering machine. He was a priest with no housekeeper, rattling around in that big old ark all by himself. Say what you might about Addie Greeno, at least in the old days when you called Father Finn, she was always present to answer the phone. Next she considered calling Frederick, who, like Janet, was sure to offer her a flattering dose of encouragement, but her bedside clock told her that he'd already left for work. Besides, the last time she'd called him, Lee Ann Raft had answered the phone, and Agatha was embarrassed to talk to her because she suspected that Lee Ann and Frederick were cohabiting. She dialed Harriet's number and then hung up immediately, remembering that Harriet slept late in the morning.

So she phoned John Beezer.

"Mr. Beezer, I have your granddaughter in my apartment."

"Jennie? You got Jennie at your place?"

"She's been here since yesterday afternoon."

"Well now, tell me, Missus, what's going on? I see you and Ernie and the girl for half a minute at supper last night, but when I come out of the dining room, you all three disappeared."

"Ernie went off to find his car. It seems the Hillyard boy stole it."

"Oh, oh. And if I know Ernie, he hasn't told the cops. He's trying to get his car back all by hisself."

"He can hardly tell the police, because he's a felon. He kidnapped this little girl."

"Naw, that's no felon offense; that's his own kid."

"It's a serious crime, Mr. Beezer."

"Naw, it's his ex-wife who's to blame. She kept holding the kid back from Ernie."

"Two wrongs don't make a right."

"They don't?" John Beezer sounded perplexed. "You mean Ernie's in trouble even if his ex-wife's to blame?"

"Of course he is."

"Dang."

He fell silent then, and Agatha said good-bye and hung up.

She set up the TV table again and brought Jennie a bowl of cornflakes she'd prepared with milk and sugar. At a commercial interruption in the cartoons, she asked the girl about her mother. "Do you miss her?"

This was obviously the wrong question for Jennie looked at her and began to whimper.

"Does your mother work?"

The girl nodded. "At the turkey plant."

"Is she a good mother to you?"

Jennie nodded again, and added, "But not to my sisters."

Agatha hid her surprise. "How many sisters do you have?"

"Two."

"Are they older or younger than you?"

"One's about thirteen and one's about eleven."

"And does your father see *them* on weekends?"

The girl shook her head. "He don't wanna."

"And why doesn't he want to see them?"

Jennie looked at Agatha as if she were dotty. "Cuz he's not their daddy." Another cartoon appeared and distracted the girl.

John Beezer came calling. Agatha asked him in for a cup of coffee and excused herself to get dressed. Settled at the kitchen table, he shouted into the bedroom, "You heard from my boy yet, Missus?"

"No," she called. "He said he'd be back shortly, but he's been gone all night."

"Wonder where he's got to?"

When she emerged, dressed in her best blue suit with her diamond brooch pinned to her lapel, John Beezer said, "So Ernie's in trouble with the law, you say?"

"Of course he is. You can't go around stealing children from their homes. I wouldn't be surprised if he gets prison time for what he's done."

Just then the phone rang and she hurried into the bedroom to answer it.

"Miss McGee?" A man's voice.

"Yes."

"This is Ernie Beezer; I'm in jail. That sumbitch is gone with my car and I'm coolin' my heels in jail."

"Well, that's what comes from kidnapping, Mr. Beezer. I was just telling your father that you'll be lucky to stay out of prison."

"You got my dad there?"

"Yes, he's in the other room."

"Let me talk to him."

On her way to the kitchen she said, "Now you'll no doubt need a lawyer, Mr. Beezer. I recommend Mr. Caferty here in Staggerford."

"I already got one—Sam Walters, here in Bartlett."

John Beezer took the telephone, laughing at first, obviously happy to hear his son's voice, then grew serious as he listened, saying very little, only a grunt of assent now and then. Finally he asked, "You want to talk to her?"

Agatha took the phone and said, "Yes?"

"Jennie?"

"Oh no, sorry, here she is." She carried the telephone to the girl, whose eyes brightened momentarily at the sound of her father's voice. She said yeah a couple of times and then grew weary of listening when a colorful new cartoon came on the TV.

"Ernie never shoulda went to the cops," his father told Agatha after the call was finished.

"Did he tell you how he came to be arrested so soon?"

"Yeah, he went to the sister's place of the sumbitch that stole his Buick and he didn't see the car, so he had Calvin Christianson drive him out to the farm. He got in his pickup and went to the cops in Bartlett, and they arrested him the minute he come through the door. They had just got in a brand-new poster with his picture on it and they recognized him as the father of the missing kid. See, his ex-wife, she reported that her daughter'd been kidnapped and she thought Ernie probably done it. Her name's Beatrice. She hasn't got any respect for Ernie, never did have."

"Maybe she has good reason."

"He said they're still looking for the kid. He said we better keep her here till he gets out."

"Goodness, that could be years."

"Naw, he's getting out today. He's got a buddy who's a bail bondsman. He'll put up the money to get him out."

Agatha, beside herself with worry, decided that the minute John Beezer left she would call the police. But John Beezer didn't leave. In order to take her mind off the dire situation, she decided to correct his grammar. "Mr. Beezer, do you realize there's a perfectly good past tense for *come*? It's *came,* but you never use it."

He gave her a puzzled look.

"I realize it's hard to break the habits of a lifetime, but you said you *come* out of the dining room last night. You should have said you *came* out of the dining room last night."

He asked why.

"Because there's a right way of speaking and a wrong way of speaking."

"There is?"

She looked at him closely to see if he was pulling her leg, but he seemed truly never to have heard of such a concept as faulty grammar.

He looked at the floor and smiled a little as he tried out the right way, saying under his breath, "I came out of the dining room last night." He repeated it and then raised his eyes and asked, "What else?"

"I can't think at the moment, but if you want me to, I can make notes of the other wrong things you say. Now if you will excuse me, I have some work to attend to."

He rose from his chair obediently.

She suggested, "Maybe you want to take the girl with you?"

"Naw, she's fine where she is." On his way out of her apartment he stepped over and fondly mussed the girl's hair. Then he left.

The phone rang as Agatha was about to pick it up. It was Mayor Mulholland returning her call.

Agatha told him why she'd called. He said it was a matter for the police. "That's why I'm calling you, because I want you to tell the police."

"Why me?" he asked, even though he knew it would be useless to argue.

"Because I need a go-between, somebody I can talk to. I don't know any of Staggerford's policemen anymore."

"You know Duane Calder. He was in your class a couple of years after me."

"Duane Calder is too stupid to understand English. I would like you to talk to the chief of police."

"Duane Calder *is* chief."

"Heaven forbid, how did that happen?"

"The town council appointed him."

"Goodness, how dreadful for our town. Anyhow, you have the information you need: the girl Jennie Beezer is here at Sunset Senior Apartments and her father will be coming for her sometime today."

Agatha hung up and was surprised to discover herself hoping that Ernie would show up before the police.

She heard a conversation in the hall. John Beezer telling Calvin Christianson all about it.

"You mean the kid is in there with Miss McGee?" said Calvin.

"Yep, watching TV with the new woman."

"Well, how is she related?"

"I told you—she's my granddaughter."

"No, I mean the new woman."

"Oh, she ain't related. Ernie just left the kid with her."

"Sounds like Ernie's had himself quite a time since I left him off at the farm last night."

"Ernie'll be fine. He's coming back today for his daughter."

"That is, if he gets out of jail."

"Oh, he'll get out of jail all right." John Beezer's voice faded down the hallway. "Ernie knows the right people."

There came a knock on Agatha's door. It was Calvin, who told her, "You know I was a deputy sheriff once and I remember the time I was called out to help search for a lost kid who turned out to have been kidnapped by his daddy. Yeah, we spent the whole day searching the eighty acres next to the farm where the kid lived with his mother."

"I'm sure that won't be necessary in this case," said Agatha. "I've told the authorities where the girl is."

"Yeah, well, it had rained the morning we searched for the kid, and so the underbrush and grass were all wet. We had a miserable time of it, and wasn't the sheriff hoppin' mad when he found out that the kid was safe and sound with his daddy down in Minneapolis? He cussed a blue streak."

"Not very edifying in an elected official," said Agatha, quite bored by Calvin.

"Oh, he was the cussingest man I ever knew. Why, he knew more cusswords than you ever heard in your life."

"It's a shame the way people like that are put into public office." She suppressed a yawn, then added, "Here in Staggerford we have a chief of police who's an idiot."

Calvin took exception to this opinion. "Duane Calder? No, no, Missus McGee, Duane's a great policeman. He's the guy who stopped the holdup in the 7-Eleven last month."

"I am *Miss* McGee, not Missus."

"So this is the granddaughter," he said, turning his attention to Jennie.

"Yes, Jennie, say hello to Mr. Christianson."

Jennie, either not hearing Agatha or choosing to ignore her, kept her eyes on the screen, where Martha Stewart was chopping celery.

"That's okay," said Calvin, "Jennie doesn't feel like saying hello to an old man." He sat down next to the girl in front of the television and watched silently as Martha Stewart's spatula spread celery around a sauté pan.

Agatha went to the kitchen sink and washed the two coffee cups and the cereal bowl, growing more agitated by the minute. She felt she must do something, rather than merely wait for either Ernie or the police to show up.

After Martha Stewart signed off, Calvin finally went back to his own apartment and Agatha grew even more nervous. Waiting helplessly for something to happen felt like being inside a pressure cooker. Agatha, a preemptive woman, a woman of action, needed to act.

She decided that she herself must return the girl to her mother. She called Calvin Christianson and asked if he would drive her to Bartlett.

He said he'd be happy to.

"I'd ask my grandnephew, but he's at work."

"Forget about your nephew, Miss McGee. Any time you need anything, just come to Calvin."

"All right, I'll get the girl ready and we'll go."

Realizing that Jennie had no coat, she went to her closet and brought out a sweater of her own, which Jennie didn't approve of. She screamed when Agatha put it on over her pink dress. Agatha screamed back, "Stop it!" and the girl fell silent, looking at her for a moment in disbelief, then raised her fist to hit her, but Agatha stopped her with her most teacherly tone: "Listen here, young lady, I'm eighty-seven, which is much too old to put up with your tantrums. You'll recall that I didn't ask you to come here, and if I hear one more peep out of you, I'll throw you out into the snow."

Jennie lowered her hand and began to whimper.

"And stop that whining!" Agatha ordered. "If there's anything worse than a tantrum, it's sniveling like that."

The girl held her expression of abject sadness as Agatha took her hand and followed Calvin out to his car, a big, old, expensive-looking Chevrolet. The day was warm. Melting snow ran in the streets.

21

O nce he got out onto the open highway, Calvin said more about his days at the sheriff's office in Rookery. He talked of arsonists and rapists, robbers and con men. Agatha interrupted him from the backseat to ask if he had ever known a criminal named Kirk Hillyard.

"Name sounds familiar."

"He's Mrs. Hillyard's son. You've seen him with her at Friday coffee. She comes from Rookery."

"So that's who that guy was." Calvin hit his forehead with the flat of his hand. "I knew I'd seen him somewhere. He used to steal money from stores in Rookery. 'Course, the city itself was out of our jurisdiction—we handled stuff outside the city limits—but sure, I used to see his picture in the newspaper. He got himself arrested about once a month, it seemed. I think he was finally sent up the river for dealing drugs."

"That's the man all right. And now he's stolen Ernie Beezer's car."

"Why, that son of a gun," said Calvin as they entered Bartlett, a town of three hundred people. "I knew Ernie was looking for his car, but he never said who took it."

Agatha said to the girl beside her, "Show us where you live, Jennie."

The girl sat up to look out the front and pointed straight ahead. At the town's only stoplight, she pointed right and Calvin drove along a short street of neatly kept houses and yards until he was out in the country again.

"I know the way from here," Calvin said. "I brought her daddy out here last night to get his truck." Beside a mailbox with BEEZER lettered on it, he turned in at a long dirt driveway. "Around here they haven't got near the snow we have," he added.

Agatha knew this was the girl's father's home and not her mother's—her mother lived in town—but she held her tongue because she was curious to see the farm. The driveway ran along a snowless hillside pasture facing the sun where a small herd of cows—some lying down, some standing—stared at them as they passed. They came to a barn that was losing its red paint and leaning south. Past a corncrib and a machine shed they came to the house, the best-looking building on the farm. It was a square frame house, two stories and painted white. Quickly Jennie jumped from the car and started walking around the corner of the house.

"Catch her!" Agatha told Calvin, who opened his door and went after her. Agatha followed at a slower pace, carefully stepping around puddles. She saw, on the back stoop, that Calvin had a tight grip on the girl, who was screaming and kicking. Agatha was about to scold her again when another vehicle came splashing into the yard.

Jennie, recognizing the white pickup, yelled, "That's my daddy!" and Calvin let her go. She ran to the truck as Ernie climbed out and took her up in his arms. With his free hand he picked a cell phone out of his pickup, punched a number and asked the operator to ring the Bartlett police station. Waiting, he gave Calvin and Agatha a little smile and said, "The cops are looking for Jennie over at your place in Staggerford. Somebody musta tipped 'em off." Then he said into the telephone, "You can call off your search for my daughter. She's safe with me now. Well, who the hell do you think it is? It's Ernie Beezer." He clicked off the phone and dropped it into his shirt pocket. "There," he said. "That's taken care of."

It was quite chilly standing in the shadow of the house. "My feet are cold," said Agatha, turning to get back into the Chevrolet. She added, "She's all yours, Mr. Beezer. You'd better take her back to her mother, or we can take her."

"Naw, possession is nine tenths of the law, remember."

"And another thing," she told him, "I wonder if your cows should be out in the pasture. It's still winter, you know."

Ernie was suddenly amused, as if being advised on farmwork by an old lady was the funniest thing that had ever happened to him. He let out a voluminous laugh that echoed in the farmyard as Agatha climbed into the passenger side of the front seat.

The two men said more to each other, then Calvin got in behind the wheel. "He said it's a neighbor who let the cows out. The neighbor comes over and milks them when Ernie's gone." In turning the car around, he backed across the driveway and Agatha told him to stop right there. She rolled down her window and called to Ernie, who was about to disappear around the corner of the house. "We'll wait here and follow you into town, Mr. Beezer. There's no hurry."

She told Calvin to leave the car where it was, blocking the driveway. He refrained from telling her he thought she was crazy, sitting out here in this farmyard when it was nearly time for lunch.

"Can you get a bit more heat out of the heater?" she asked, and he fiddled with the controls. She hadn't worn her boots and her feet were still cold.

After two minutes of silence, Calvin said, "If we start back now, we can just make lunch." When she didn't respond, he decided to point out the uselessness of sitting here. "You're bluffing of course. You know he'll probably never come out of that house. We could be waiting here all day."

"You're right, Calvin, I am bluffing, but on the other hand, I have a notion about the man. He's compulsive. Look at this yard. There isn't a scrap of junk anywhere, and all of his machinery is under a roof. I'm guessing that he'll need to clear us out of his driveway before long."

"But *how* long? I'm mighty hungry."

"Within the hour. We can ask Little Edna to make you a sandwich when we get back."

"An hour's too long. I'm driving out of here in exactly fifteen minutes."

"Forty-five minutes," she said.

Only seven minutes passed before Ernie came around the corner of his house and stood at Calvin's window. "Go on home now, you two. If you're waitin' for me, I'm not goin' anyplace." He turned to go back inside.

Agatha got out and called to him. He turned and she asked him, "Will you at least tell us where your ex-wife lives?"

"Turn left at the stoplight," he said. "She's the third house on your right. Be careful; she's a hellcat." He disappeared back around the corner.

She saw Jennie watching from the front window. She waved at her and got back into the car.

"All right, we can go," she told Calvin. "Turn left at the stoplight in town and stop at the third house on our right."

"Why?" he asked, putting the car in gear.

"Because I need to take the measure of the girl's mother. I mean, there might be a good reason why the girl prefers her father."

At the stoplight he turned and drove past several stores. When he came to houses, he slowed down, muttering, "I'd say it's none of our business."

Agatha's silence seemed to leave him no choice but to stop at the third place, a small house with a shiny coat of yellow paint. She got out and went to the front door. She knocked twice before a scrawny red-faced teenager opened the door, a girl who must have been one of Jennie's half sisters, maybe the older one. "Is your mother home?" Agatha asked.

The girl nodded and stood aside to let her into a tiny living room where a long-haired boy sat on the couch, gingerly running his fingertips over the pimples on his face. Agatha said, "How do you do?" but the boy, with his eyes on the girl, said nothing.

The girl went to a dark doorway off the living room, called, "Ma, there's somebody here," and sat down next to the boy, who draped his arm across her shoulders.

"Shouldn't you be in school?" asked Agatha.

"It's lunch hour," said the girl.

Agatha heard the creak of bedsprings in the darkened room and soon a scowling, wild-haired woman emerged with a threatening look on her face. "Hell of a note how a woman can't take a decent nap in this house." She was looking at Agatha as she said this. She was thin and haggard. Her expression of displeasure deepened when she discovered the long-haired boy sitting on the couch. "Git out of here, you bastard," she said to him. He didn't move and she raised her voice, "Git out now, Harold. I won't have you in here feeling up my daughters." She stepped over to the couch and slapped both of them hard on the face. The girl protested, crying, "We didn't do nothing, Ma." The boy just laughed. The woman then turned to Agatha, who was opening the front door. She went after her and laid a hand on her shoulder, saying, "Who are you and what do you want?"

Agatha turned to face her. Close up, she saw what might have been craziness in the woman's eyes, certainly it was profound unhappiness. She said, "Never mind, I've seen enough," and she let herself out. Returning to the car she made a mental note to add the occupants of this house to her prayer list.

Calvin said, "Well?"

"We'll go home now and ask Little Edna for that sandwich."

Calvin had scarcely put the car in gear when Agatha told him, "No, turn around and go back to the corner."

"What for?"

"I saw a telephone booth there."

Calvin obeyed, making a U-turn and parking next to the booth. When Agatha made no move to get out of the car, he said, "Now what?"

"I wonder if you'd be so kind as to look up an address in the telephone book? I'd do it myself but I'm exhausted." As Calvin opened his door, she added, "Laurie Hillyard is the name."

He was gone only a few moments. He opened his door and said, "There's no book in there." He didn't get in because he knew he wasn't finished doing her bidding.

"Well then," she said, "ask the operator."

He went back and did so. He got back in the car without saying anything. He drove to the east end of town and stopped before a small, brown, one-story house. "This place looks familiar," he said. "I think I was here last night too."

Agatha opened her door and struggled, but failed, to stand up. Calvin, pitying her, asked if he should go to the door with a message of some sort.

"No," she said, she had to go herself. But if he'd be so kind as to help her get to her feet . . .

He went around the car and set her on her feet, noticing that she weighed scarcely more than a pair of cigars.

"Old age certainly has nothing to recommend it, Calvin."

"Oh, I don't know—when I think how much wiser I've become over the years."

"You're saying that proves how young you are?"

"I'm seventy-two," he said proudly.

"Wait until you're eighty-seven and see how you feel."

He helped her almost to the door, then retreated to the car. She pressed the doorbell and heard a clanging of chimes inside.

She pressed it two or three more times before giving up and walking around to the back of the house, looking for signs of life. She saw a two-car garage off the alley and she tried the door. It opened. She stepped inside hoping to see Ernie Beezer's Buick, but it contained a small black sportscar. On the floor she saw a pair of license plates and a screwdriver. She returned to Calvin's car. This time he held the door for her and lifted her by the elbow.

"Next we'll find Bartlett's elementary school," she said in the confident tone of one used to being obeyed.

Calvin didn't obey. Although he'd never been her student at St. Isidore's (his parents had been Protestants), he'd known Agatha all his life, had known of her imperious ways, and he was curious to know what she'd do if someone didn't follow her directions. He headed out of town.

What she did, at the edge of Bartlett, was to grab the steering wheel and tug it to the right so that the Chevrolet ran up on the sidewalk before he regained control of it. He looked at her in disbelief—she could have caused an accident. She was looking straight ahead with a small smile playing on her lips. She said, "Jennie told me her school is near the post office, wherever that is."

Calvin drove back to the stoplight, turned left and came upon the post office and next to it, the school. Valentine's Day being the next big holiday of the year, they saw hearts and similar cutouts pasted in the windows of a classroom. Again Calvin helped Agatha out of the car and along the sidewalk to the entrance. "Come in with me, if you please," she said, and he did. They went through a doorway marked PRINCIPAL, where Agatha interrupted a conversation between two secretaries to ask where Laurie Hillyard's classroom was.

"Down that way, 103," one of them said, and they both pointed.

Peering through the small window in the door of 103,

Agatha saw Laurie, wearing jeans, writing on the blackboard while her students caused trouble. Many were up out of their chairs and moving about at will. One blew a spitball through a straw and hit a girl in the nape of the neck. Two boys wrestled at the back of the room. It was too noisy for Agatha's knock to be heard, so she opened the door and called to Laurie, who turned with a puzzled look.

"We've met in Staggerford at coffee time," Agatha explained, but this did nothing to relieve Laurie of her confusion, so she added, "Sunset Senior Apartments."

Laurie understood. "We're busy at the moment," she said, "but what can I do for you?"

"I'd ask you to get your class to quiet down, but that would be useless. I'm here to inquire about your brother Kirk."

A look of distaste stole over her face at the mention of his name. "What about him?"

"Where is he?"

She shrugged, "I don't know and I don't care. Why do you ask?"

"Because he stole a car and he probably stole your license plates. Do you know your license number?"

"Ah, 122-something."

They were distracted by a cry of pain from one of the wrestling boys. Laurie went to the back of the room to separate them and Agatha went in and stood in front of the blackboard, facing the mostly empty chairs. She clapped her hands until most of the students grew silent and faced her. She said, "Class, take your seats." When she saw how bewildered they all looked, she realized they hadn't been assigned desks. "All right, then sit down in any chair." They did. "Now I want to tell you a story about a student I had many years ago named Samuel."

"Samuel the spaniel," said a boy on Agatha's right and several students laughed. She glared at him until he had to look away. She then glared at each child in turn—twenty-two of them—as she continued her story.

"His name was Samuel Johanson and he came from a well-to-do family. Samuel was very bright. I was told he had an IQ above a hundred and fifty. He was especially good at science. One year when he was a high school student he built a rocket and launched it up miles in the air, almost high enough to go into orbit. But Samuel had a flaw as a student. Even when he was a sixth grader, in my classroom, I suspected that he would come to grief unless he learned to shut his mouth. For his flaw, you see, was that he talked incessantly. He never paid attention to what was told to him."

She looked from face to face before her. All of them, including Laurie Hillyard, standing at the back of the room, were giving her their rapt attention, except the boy who'd said Samuel the spaniel—he was turned around and whispering to the boy behind him.

"Come here," Agatha said to him. "Yes, you, come up here to the front." She turned an empty chair around and placed him on it, facing his classmates. "Think of this young man as a kind of symbol, class. Let him stand for Samuel, because although he looks nothing like him, he behaves like Samuel."

She paused to gather her strength and the room burst into laughter, apparently caused by a face the boy was making, so Agatha turned his chair around so they could see only the back of his head, and she continued:

"It was Samuel's ambition to go to medical school and become a doctor. His father was Dr. Johanson, who expected his son to join him in his clinic and practice medicine with him. Well, Samuel graduated from Staggerford High School with an undistinguished record and he never got his premed degree. You see, he proved to be a hopeless student in college despite his potential. He didn't pay attention in class. He was never able to quiet down and study. Nowadays they have a term for such behavior, attention deficit disorder, but whatever you call it, it destroyed Samuel's ambition to become a doctor. The last I heard he was living as a street person in Minneapolis. So I leave you with—"

"That boy needs a dose of Ritalin," said the boy in the chair.

Half the class laughed hysterically; the other half said, "Shhh," for they wanted to hear what the old lady would leave them with.

"I leave you with this thought," she said. "When I saw the way you were behaving while Miss Hillyard wrote on the board, it looked to me as if you all had attention deficit disorder."

Leaving the classroom, she took the arm of Calvin Christianson for support. She couldn't remember ever being so exhausted. The motion of the Chevrolet put her immediately to sleep and she slept soundly until Calvin woke her as he pulled up in front of Sunset Senior.

22

⌒⌒⌒

Agatha found Little Edna in her kitchen and asked if Calvin might be fed.

"Sure," said Little Edna. "I can make you both a ham sandwich and coleslaw." She seemed agitated.

"Not me," said Agatha. "I need a good sleep more than anything. We've been to Bartlett."

"Well, while you were in Bartlett, we had the police here," Edna said. "They searched every room, including yours." Joe came shuffling in from another room and added, "They had a warrant and they forced me to unlock every door where nobody was home and they looked under everybody's bed. For some reason they thought the Beezer girl was here."

Agatha left Calvin in the Rinkwitzes' kitchen, munching on his sandwich and telling them about his days as deputy sheriff. She hurried to her apartment, went straight to the phone and got Ernie Beezer's number from the operator. When he answered she said, "I have been to your ex-wife's house and I see why your daughter prefers your company, Mr. Beezer. Now the first thing we must do is clear your name."

"Naw, that's okay, Miss McGee. Everybody knows Jennie's safe with me."

"No, you've been charged with a crime, and you will be brought to trial. Surely you were told that when you were released from jail."

"Sure, I've got to go to a hearing in the county seat next month, but it won't amount to a hill of beans. Possession is nine tenths of the law."

Agatha wanted to call him stupid for repeating this meaningless phrase, but she restrained herself and asked how Jennie was.

"Jennie's fine. She's takin' a nap. She's had a busy couple days."

"All right, Mr. Beezer, stay in touch."

She switched on her telephone answering device and heard Harriet's voice asking where Agatha had been and adding that she missed seeing her. Then John Beezer came on, asking if Agatha had any new words for him to study. It took her a moment to remember that she had risked his displeasure by correcting his grammar, and yet, far from being offended, he was asking for more of the same. She was touched.

Agatha pulled down the window shades, darkening the room, and lay down on her couch, ready for a nap, but then she realized it was almost time for Friday coffee. She considered not going, but couldn't resist—coffee time was always so full of interesting gossip. She went to her dressing table and prepared her face for the dining room, where she sat a few minutes later between Harriet and John Beezer. The police visit had made Agatha the center of attention. Women at the other tables, whom she was gradually beginning to know by name, kept looking at her. She told Harriet that she had seen her son Kirk the afternoon before, when he'd dropped the girl off at her apartment. Harriet said, "Yes, he called me this morning and told me."

"Oh, where did he call from?"

"Minneapolis. He's loved the city ever since we lived there. He was pretty small when we moved to Rookery—I think he was only eight—but he still goes to the city every chance he gets."

Agatha was tempted to reveal to her that her son was a car thief, but she didn't want to see any more of the woman's tears.

John Beezer asked, "Ain'tcha got any more words for me, Missus?"

"Yes, I have—*ain't*. We don't say *ain't* in polite company." He looked proudly at Big Edna and Addie across the table, as if to say, *Lookit here, I'm takin' language lessons from the new woman.*

"And *ain'tcha got* is substandard," she added. "You should say *Don't you have* instead. You have to enunciate clearly. *'Don't. You. Have.'* "

"Don't you have," he said a couple of times under his breath.

Addie said to him, "Mr. Beezer, I hear your son has a new girlfriend."

Agatha was puzzled by the guilty look he shot her before he nodded and said, "That's a fact."

"Edna here says it was the girl he met at Agatha's house at Christmas dinner."

What girl, thought Agatha. She didn't remember a girl at her table. "Who is it?" she asked John Beezer.

Big Edna answered for him. "It's the Raft girl."

"Lee Ann," added Addie.

No, thought Agatha, Lee Ann Raft was Frederick's fiancée. She said, "Lee Ann Raft is no girl. She's forty if she's a day. You must mean her sister Karen."

But both women insisted it was Lee Ann, and John Beezer confirmed it.

Back in her apartment, Agatha phoned Mayor Mulholland and told him that Kirk Hillyard was in Minneapolis driving a car with a license plate that began with 122. Then she finally lay down for her nap. She awoke an hour later with her conscience playing guiltily over the kidnapping. She felt as if she'd been ignoring the magnitude of what she'd done, harboring the missing girl in her apartment, and now advising Ernie Beezer to keep her. She phoned her pastor, Father Healy, to tell him she was coming to see him, but first she called her house, assuming Frederick was home from work.

He said, "Hullo."

"Frederick, how are you?"

"Not so hot. I've caught a cold or something." His low-octane voice sounded as if he were losing altitude, skimming the waves over the Slough of Despond.

"Frederick, I'm told that Lee Ann is no longer in your life."

"Who told you that?"

"I heard it at coffee, a few hours ago."

A long pause. "Well, you heard right."

Agatha heard a catch in his voice. She feared the worst for him. He didn't have a jolly nature in the best of times, and this might set him off down some terrible path—depression or drugs or suicide. She said, "How are you taking it?"

"I'm doing okay."

"I worry about you, Frederick. Come see me tomorrow, won't you?"

"Saturday? Sure. What time?"

"Come in the morning. You can drive me downtown to see Judge Caferty."

She put on her coat and overshoes and walked the block to the rectory. She rang the doorbell and pushed open the heavy door of what had been the Mraz mansion. The two Mraz brothers had been pioneers and the first bankers in Staggerford. An unmarried granddaughter of one of the bankers—Ann Mraz was her name and she'd been a friend of Agatha's—had willed the house to the church.

Stepping inside, she caught a whiff of popcorn. Father Healy was evidently having an early supper. His eating habits were scandalous—that was one topic that Agatha and Addie Greeno agreed on. She found him in the kitchen sharing a dishpanful of popcorn with Leonard Fossum, St. Isidore's lazy but cheerful handyman. Both men stood when they saw Agatha. She put out her hand to shake, to avoid being kissed. Father Healy, a hearty man in his early sixties, had developed the habit of greeting women by kissing them on the cheek.

Leonard Fossum shook it first, briefly, saying "mum," and then quickly dropped it and sat down.

"Sorry, Miss McGee," said the priest, taking his turn. "I didn't hear you knock."

"I didn't knock; I rang your doorbell."

"Oh, that doesn't work; you have to knock. Leonard, I wonder if you'd see to the doorbell."

"Sure thing," said Leonard, making no move to leave the kitchen. "First thing tomorrow."

"No, I mean now, please, because Agatha and I have to talk."

"Go right ahead," said Leonard, stuffing more popcorn into his mouth and still not rising from his chair. "Don't mind me."

"Privately," added the priest.

Leonard finally understood. He took a bowl from the cupboard, loaded it with popcorn and went into the front room, where they soon heard the television blaring.

"So, how was your day?" asked Father Healy.

"Busy," said Agatha. "I've been involved in a kidnapping."

The priest, as she expected, looked amused. It was a habit worse than kissing women on the cheek, this way he had of looking amused every time Agatha came to him with something serious. But she hid her disgust and went on:

"There was a five- or six-year-old little girl taken from her home in Bartlett yesterday," she began.

"Yes, it was on the radio. Don't tell me you took her."

"No, but I harbored her all yesterday and through the night."

"Well, I'm sure you had good reason."

"My reasons improved today when I saw where the child lived, but that doesn't change the fact that I took part in a crime, does it?"

"Tell me why you took part."

"The child was brought to my apartment. It seemed the kidnapper was in a hurry and dropped her off with me because the person he was supposed to leave her with wasn't home."

"Well, there you are," said the priest.

"And what is that supposed to mean?"

"I mean there's your reason, your excuse. You were a victim of circumstances."

"But I didn't tell the authorities until this morning, and then I took the girl away so they wouldn't find her in my apartment. No, that isn't true exactly. I took the girl to Bartlett intending to return her to her mother. But then I met the mother—she's slatternly, Father, absolutely a slattern, and I left the girl at her father's farm, and I told him not to return her."

"The mother knew you had the girl?"

"No, she didn't."

"Who else knew?"

"Well, the father and the kidnapper—and my neighbor Mr. Christianson."

"Wait a minute, the news said the father was the kidnapper."

"He's the force behind it certainly, but he hired another man actually to take the girl."

"And where is the other man?"

"Only the Lord knows. He's long gone. He stole the father's automobile and drove away."

"Do you know the man?"

"Yes, he's the son of a friend of mine."

Father Healy shocked Agatha by emitting a loud laugh. He said, "So you *have* fallen among thieves."

Ignoring this, she said, "What I'm here about is my part in the kidnapping, Father."

"And you want to know if it's a sin."

"Surely it is."

"Well, I have good news for you and bad news. The good

news is that it's not a sin. You have been acting according to your good instincts, and—"

"How do you know that?"

"I know it because I know you, Miss McGee. Your conscience wouldn't permit you to commit a sin."

She started to object, but all she got out was the word "But" before he raised his hand to stop her.

"Let me finish, please. The bad news is that you're probably in trouble with the law. You see, what you've done, although not immoral, is illegal. There's a distinct difference."

"So what do I do about that?"

"I don't know—I'm not a lawyer. I only deal in morality."

He didn't mean this to be dismissive, but Agatha took it that way. Stepping over to his kitchen range, he said, "Let me make you a cup of tea." But when he turned back to the table, she was gone.

As she strode though the front room, Leonard Fossum, lying on the couch with the empty popcorn bowl on his chest, took his eyes from the TV for a moment and asked, "Where you off to, Miss McGee?"

"To jail in all likelihood, according to the good father," she said, "but heaven thereafter."

Walking back to her apartment with her scarf over her mouth because it had turned very cold, she went over the priest's words in her mind, and thought he might be right. If she had not sinned, she faced the more immediate problem of protecting herself from the police. She would consult Judge Caferty when Frederick took her to his office first thing in the morning.

23

When Frederick arrived the next morning, Agatha began by asking, "How's your work going?"

"Good," he said. His eyes looked bleary, as if he'd been weeping.

"Any new people on your mail route?"

"Yep, two since last week."

"Oh? Anybody I'd know?"

"One's named Varney; the other's named Steinbrenner."

It wasn't easy getting to the heart of Frederick, but Agatha was used to trying. It was a matter of breaking him down with small talk.

"How are the water pipes in the house?" she asked.

"Pipes are fine. 'Course we haven't had below-zero weather since Thanksgiving."

Ah, he was beginning to open up, offering two sentences in the same reply. She pressed him further, asking about her old neighbors the Rathmanns and the Demings.

"They're doing fine, at least as far as I know," he said. He told her of Mr. Rathmann's retirement from the feed mill. He said the Rathmanns were spending the winter in Arizona. As for the Demings, Mr. Deming was still driving out to his farm every day, even in winter, when there was nothing to do out there but maybe plow the snow off the driveway. Mrs. Deming had brought Frederick a peach pie recently that was very delicious.

Next, Agatha decided to tenderize him by throwing in a little self-pity. He listened attentively as she told him about her involvement with the missing Beezer girl. She said she was particularly worried about it because she didn't know how much longer she would live—her mortality had been much on her mind lately—and she didn't want the kidnapping to be her last act on earth.

"Speaking of mortality," said Frederick, "did you hear that Father Healy has cancer?"

This brought her up short. Father Healy has cancer? What was God thinking, with the worldwide shortage of priests? "No, I hadn't heard that. I just spoke with him yesterday. Perhaps it's a false rumor."

"Maybe," said Frederick deferentially.

"Frederick, I'm sorry to pry, but I have to ask you about Lee Ann. What happened?"

He shifted uncomfortably in his chair. "I guess she fell for somebody else."

"Do you know who?"

He nodded. "The little Beezer girl's father. She met him at Christmas dinner." He looked at the floor.

"Oh my goodness—the day Lillian died. What a terrible Christmas that was."

"Terrible all right," he said, nodding again, his eyes on his shoes.

"I didn't approve of your living together, of course, but I have to say I rather liked Lee Ann. I had hoped you'd marry."

"You did?" He looked genuinely surprised.

"Yes, I did. I hate to see you go through life alone."

This admission broke a dam of some sort in Frederick. Twenty minutes had been enough time to cut through the formalities and lay bare his grief. He said everything seemed gray since Lee Ann had left him; there was no color in life anymore. The habits he used to enjoy—lunching at Kruger's Pool Hall, pausing in his mail route to take in the vista from Substation Hill—gave him no pleasure anymore. He said everything was such hard work these days.

"What things?" asked Agatha.

"Oh, you know. Getting up in the morning to go to work. Washing my clothes. Everything."

She looked at his clothes; his tan shirt and pants weren't clean.

He added, "I don't suppose you've ever felt this way?"

"Of course I have," she said. "You don't get to be eighty-seven without experiencing depression a time or two. Two months ago, when I moved in here, why do you think I moved back to the house right away?"

Again surprised. "You were depressed?"

"Of course I was depressed."

"But you didn't show it."

"Well, it's a wonder—I certainly felt it." She thought back nearly twenty years to a more serious case of depression, the summer she had come home from her first trip to Ireland, having discovered that James O'Hannon, the man she loved, was a priest. She recalled how all the color and joy had gone out of her life. She was lucky that Bishop Baker had offered her the principalship of St. Isidore's Elementary, because once school started in the fall she threw herself into her work and her malaise disappeared.

But Frederick had no new job to take his mind off his problem. She said, "I think you should see Dr. Hammond about this."

"Naw, what can he do?"

"He can prescribe medicine to make you feel better."

"Did you go to the doctor?"

"No, I kept it inside, as you are doing. But I've heard it said that talking about it can help. If not to a doctor, then to a support group. There must be a mental health support group some-where in town."

"I've never heard of one." Frederick looked relieved by this fact.

"I'll ask our manager, Mrs. Rinkwitz. She takes her husband to a Parkinson's support group. And now, Frederick, if you'd be so kind as to take me down to Judge Caferty's office."

"Sure," he said, jingling his car keys. "I'm parked out in front."

"All right, just give me a minute to talk to Mrs. Rinkwitz and then we'll go."

"Good," he said. While she was gone down the hall, he turned on her TV and stared at a talk show without really hear-ing it. He was thinking back twenty-five years to the night in Saigon when the girl he'd met in a bar was taking him home with her. He was so happy he could hardly contain himself. He thought she was beautiful—her big eyes, her pitch-black hair piled up behind her head. He had planned to bring her to the States and marry her. Why not? Others had done the same thing. They turned a dark corner and she had run ahead, teasing him, and was blown apart by the grenade that came sailing in from out of nowhere. This memory had haunted him over the years, but he hadn't brought it to mind once since Lee Ann Raft moved in with him. He wept briefly in Agatha's apartment over losing both women, the girl in Vietnam as well as Lee Ann.

Judge Caferty was obviously feeling jolly this morning for he chuckled under his breath as he welcomed Agatha and Freder-ick into his office. In fact, he actually took Agatha in his arms for a moment before she pushed him away.

"Well, well, well," he said as he led them into his inner office and took his place behind his desk. "I understand the exhuma-tion of Lillian Kite came off swimmingly." He waited for Agatha to agree, and when she did not, he asked, "To what do I owe the pleasure of this visit?"

"I am here to ask your advice, Maynard. I seem to have gotten myself into a peck of trouble." Agatha was sitting on the couch and Frederick stood beside her—looking emaciated, thought the judge. She reviewed for him her part in the kidnapping, which, she said, caused her to be in trouble with the law. She repeated Father Healy's words about illegality as opposed to immorality, in case the judge wasn't aware of the difference.

When she finished, he asked her an embarrassing question. Never in nine decades of life had she expected to respond to anything as humiliating as, "Have you ever been charged with a crime, Agatha?"

"No," she said weakly.

"Well then, I'd say you're being premature. Come back and see me if and when you've been charged and I'll get you off the hook. And now what do you say we imbibe in a bit of the hair of the dog?" He drew from his desk a bottle similar to the one he'd offered her last time. She shook her head and closed her eyes, and when she opened them, she beheld Frederick standing at the desk and taking a swig from the bottle.

"We really must go," she said, getting up and leading Frederick from the office.

The judge followed them out, standing at the outer door and calling after them, "Come to my house, Agatha, and play a recital. I've got a Yamaha upright I'm told has a swell sound to it."

"I'm afraid Judge Caferty is becoming a souse," said Agatha. "I wouldn't patronize him at all if he hadn't been my father's partner."

She led Frederick across the street to the bank and he followed her downstairs into the basement community room, where they found the group of Parkinson's people standing and sitting in a circle of folding chairs, slowly shedding their coats and visiting. Agatha saw the Rinkwitzes among them. She found the social worker and asked her if there was a mental health support group in town.

"Not that I know of," said the woman, "but I'll help facilitate if you want to start one."

"Oh, it isn't for me I'm asking," said Agatha. "It's for my grandnephew here, who's suffering from a case of depression."

The social worker looked closely at Frederick, which embarrassed him, and said, "Chronic or short term?"

Agatha, unsure, turned and looked him over as well. Uncomfortable as a specimen on exhibit, he settled the matter by saying, "Short term."

A freight elevator opened and the social worker hurried over to help an elderly man out into the room. Agatha stepped over to Mrs. Severson, her former student, and spoke with her until the group settled down. She took a seat. Frederick recognized a pair of men from his mail route and went and sat near them.

Again the hour consisted of a recital of symptoms. One woman had the shakes so bad, she said, that she couldn't eat and had lost another four pounds. Joe Rinkwitz said that he had fallen down more than three hundred and twenty times and had recently broken a rib. One of the men Frederick knew, a fellow named Goltz, said he was glad to hear it because he'd thought he was the only one falling down. He said he hadn't been keeping a tally, but he fell down at least once a week.

"Oh, that's nothing," said Joe, trying to keep a prideful tone out of his voice, "I'm falling almost every other day. As long as you have somebody to help you up, you're okay."

"That's the problem; I live alone," said Mr. Goltz. "It took me a quarter hour to get back on my feet the other day. See, I was out in the yard and there was nothing to grab onto."

"When I fall down, I pray it's near a chair," said Mrs. Severson. "If I have a chair handy, I can usually get up."

Mr. Goltz said the trouble was that it had started snowing

while he was on the ground. "It was Wednesday last week, the day we got that inch of snow in the morning."

Frederick, affected by the image of the old man lying helpless on the ground and covered with snow, leaned over to him and said, "If you need help, call me at the post office and I'll come out and help you up."

"Thanks, but it's not that easy. I don't usually fall near a telephone."

A man sitting opposite them said, "Out my way we never had no snow on Wednesday. We ain't had snow for two weeks."

"My deceased husband broke ribs one time by falling off a ladder," said an old woman wrapped in a black, woolly shawl such as Agatha hadn't seen since she was a girl. (James O'Hannon had had a photo of his Irish mother wrapped in a shawl like that one.) "But he didn't have Parkinson's," added the woman. "That's my first husband I'm talking about." She had a distinctive voice, but Agatha couldn't remember where she'd heard it.

Joe said that doctors couldn't do anything about broken ribs. "I hear they have to heal themselves," he said.

"Don't tell me about ribs," said Mr. Goltz. "I've had about every bone in my body broke during the war. I know about ribs."

The social worker broke in to ask if anybody in the group, or anyone they knew, would be interested in attending a mental health support group. The old lady in the shawl raised her hand and so did Mrs. Severson.

"Anybody else?" she asked.

No response.

"Well, anybody interested should see this lady here." She pointed to Agatha. "I'm sure the bank would be happy to host the meeting and you can figure out the day and time among yourselves. Just let me know when you're meeting."

Frederick was sorry to hear this. He rather liked the group he was currently in. They talked about the same things as the pool hall crowd—their ailments, the weather—and, like the pool hall crowd, they didn't pay much attention to what was said. As an army veteran himself, he wanted to ask Mr. Goltz about his wartime experience.

Toward the end of the hour when coffee was served, he turned to Goltz and said, "I never knew you were in the army."

"I wasn't. I was in the Seabees. The Seabees was a mighty dangerous outfit, which I didn't know until I joined up. Wake Island, Saipan, Okinawa, Iwo Jima—we'd go in after the first wave of marines, you know, before the island was secure, because we had to get the docks and airfields built as soon as possible."

Goltz continued, "We was shot at by the Japs and had mortar shells coming in on us while we was working. I tell you, it'd drive you nuts. One guy did go out of his mind, come to think of it. He was our first tractor driver. I was just a regular carpenter at the time. See, a mortar shell landed in front of him and two seconds later another one landed beside his tractor. He came out of it without a scratch, but he got the shakes so bad they had to send him home. He was from Kansas, as I recall.

"I took over the tractor after that, which was fine with me," said Goltz. "I always preferred not knowing when the next shell was going to hit. You'd never hear it over the sound of the tractor. You'd be working around an excavation or leveling an airfield and—bam!—a shell would go off nearby and scare the bejesus out of you. But to my mind, that was better than hearing an 'Incoming!' before it landed."

Meanwhile, Agatha was occupied by the two people interested in the mental health group: Mrs. Severson, the old woman in the shawl, and one of the men. It was determined that Monday night or Saturday afternoon would meet everyone's schedule, so she said, "All right then, we'll meet on Monday evening in the dining room of the Sunset Senior Apartments."

*   *   *

Frederick joined Agatha for Sunday dinner the next day. She was encouraged by his happier demeanor—he actually smiled now and then—and by his healthy appetite—he went back for second helpings of chicken à la king on biscuits. Mrs. Teague, who recognized him as her former mailman, came over from her table and joined them for dessert. While listening to Mrs. Teague's recital of her chores on the farm, he heard Agatha telling Harriet, on her left, about the group coming to Sunset Senior the following evening. Overhearing her, Addie and Big Edna wanted to know what she was talking about, so she repeated her announcement to them, discreetly leaving out two facts—that it was a support group and that she was doing it for Frederick's benefit.

24

On Monday evening, as a group of three visitors was gathering with Agatha, a number of residents peeked into the dining room to see what was going on. Addie Greeno actually strode in and said, "What are all these people doing here, Agatha?"

"We're meeting," she told her.

"But what for?"

"Never mind," said Agatha, hoping to spare the three poor souls the stigma attached to emotional problems.

Addie went upstairs and tattled to Big Edna, citing Agatha's incivility, and they both came down and sat at a far table in the dining room.

There was a long, uncomfortable silence as the three visitors—Frederick, Mrs. Severson and the heavy woman in the black shawl—shifted nervously in their chairs. At eight ten, Harriet came in and sat down—whether out of need or curiosity, Agatha didn't know. Finally at a quarter after eight, she announced the purpose of the meeting: to support those suffering from some form of distress. Addie Greeno immediately stood up and left the room while Big Edna came forward and joined the group.

They began by introducing themselves. Mrs. Severson said tearfully that she needed to talk about her husband Gerald, who had died a week ago. Agatha tried to tell her she had no idea and how very sorry she was, but Mrs. Severson interrupted her to say that Gerald, though a lovely man, had never made a decent living for them, had always been lazy, and sat around the house and read newspapers most of the time. He didn't have any retirement income and had sold the farm years earlier and moved into Willoughby. So, if she didn't have her freelance work as a seamstress, she'd be on the county's rolls. Mickey was a godsend, of course. Her son Mickey was an absolute lifesaver the way he kicked in to help with the rent and now and then other essentials like the phone bill and the heating bill when her work slowed down, such as now, after Christmas.

When she paused to draw a long breath, Agatha broke in to say, "We'll get back to you," and she nodded at the heavy woman in the black shawl, indicating it was her turn. This woman, seen up close, was a mess. Her hair was unclean and unkempt, lying plastered over her ears and forehead. Her eyes were bloodshot. She spoke in a measured, toneless voice, like a deaf person, and her speech was interrupted every few words by a sudden intake of breath. She said to the group, "I came tonight (hic) because I've spent the last thirty-five years in a mental hospital (hic) in St. Peter, Minnesota (hic), where we used to meet for psychotherapy twice (hic) a week, and I miss it."

The others looked at her in wonder—thirty-five years! Agatha thought of the institution she and the rest of her class had been taken to when she was a sophomore in college. It was called an insane asylum in those days and she was repulsed. She wore a red stocking cap that day for it was winter, and one of the female inmates—they were called inmates then, not residents—took a fancy to it and followed Agatha from one room to the next until finally she snatched it off her head and ran. Agatha's teacher, Father Laurentian, gave chase but lost the crazy woman in another room. He was going to report it to a guard, but Agatha asked him to forget it. She was too frightened and embarrassed to pursue the matter. The only other thing she remembered about the visit was the unwelcoming appearance of the place. All the walls were painted a uniform dingy gray and all the plumbing was visible, running outside the walls and under the ceilings. To think of spending thirty-five years in a place like that!

Agatha said, "What was the nature of your trouble, if I may ask?"

"What kind of a (hic) question is that? It's a secret and I don't have (hic) to tell any of you." The woman looked from one to another of those around the table, an intimidating glare so triumphant and haughty that it caused all the others, including Agatha, to lower their eyes. While Harriet spoke next, Agatha was preoccupied with trying to recall exactly when and where in her past she had heard the shawled woman's voice. It was so familiar, but just beyond the reach of her memory. The woman must have been a student, thought Agatha, many years ago.

When Agatha finally turned her attention to Harriet, she was happy to realize that she was speaking openly about her son Kirk. She said he was her biggest problem, had been since high school. Kirk's brother and his two sisters kept telling her to give up on him—put him out of her mind—that he was never going to change. But how do you do that? She began to weep. "How do you give up on your own flesh and blood; how do you keep yourself from going back over his boyhood day after day, looking for what you did wrong?" There was a pause and then she said, "He was arrested yesterday in Minneapolis—for car theft."

As the women spoke, Agatha noticed Frederick growing more and more agitated, and before it was Big Edna's turn he got up and left the room. She thought perhaps he was looking for a restroom and was surprised to hear the front door open and shut.

Big Edna said that weight had been a special problem of hers. It had been years since she'd weighed less than two hundred pounds. Not that it mattered anymore because now that she was elderly, her shape didn't matter so much, she was happy to say. She concluded, "I've had some minor things go wrong recently—I had a lot of dental problems and my arthritis is getting worse—but at least I don't worry about being fat anymore. I expect I'll go to my grave weighing over two hundred pounds."

"Frederick must have forgotten something at home," said Agatha, "but we'll continue anyway." She tore three pages from a notebook she'd brought along and passed them out to the three women, along with pencils. She asked them to draw a picture of the family they grew up in. "Label each person according to his or her relationship to you," she said and sat back to watch them work. She didn't tell them that this was an exercise she'd used with her sixth graders each year. She thought it would be good for these people because it never failed to reveal a lot about the artist's upbringing. Besides, freewheeling discussion had never been her strong point as a teacher. She was better at keeping her classes busy with projects such as this.

While the other two went immediately to work on their drawings, the shawled woman sat chewing on her pencil with her eyes on Agatha. After five minutes of this, she asked her, "Don't you remember your family?"

"Of course I remember," the woman shot back. "It's just that I did this pitcher so many times in the hospital that I'm sick and tired of it."

Oh my, a discipline problem, thought Agatha. She tried to think back to her days in the classroom and what she had done with students like this, but she concluded that she'd never in her long career met with such defiance. She decided to ignore her and put the group further to work.

"Now, I'd like you to turn your paper over and after putting your name at the top of the page, please describe in writing the problem you spoke about a few minutes ago."

"Hey, this ain't the way we did it in the hospital," said the discipline problem in her flat, loud voice. "We never had to write nothin'. The way psychotherapy works, it's just talkin' about stuff."

"We'll talk about 'stuff' in a few minutes," said Agatha, and she turned sideways in her chair to avoid the woman's heavy, threatening gaze.

Harriet, when the group finally got around to talking, was the first to speak about her family. "I grew up in what I guess these days you'd call a privileged household. There were six of us children and we lived on Mount Curve Avenue in Minneapolis. We had maids and we always dressed for dinner and had a fresh tablecloth every day."

Listening to her go on about her parents (her father had been a stockbroker, her mother a dear, hardworking soul who, of course, never held a job outside the home), Agatha was reminded of her own upbringing. Her own mother always seemed to be working diligently around the house—cleaning despite the maid, cooking, taking in the fresh-smelling laundry from the clothesline in the backyard. Her father was Staggerford's first attorney-at-law and, for two terms, Staggerford's first elected representative to the state legislature in St. Paul.

Mrs. Severson said that when she was still a schoolgirl, she'd lost her older sister to diphtheria and that was her first experience with death. She missed her terribly because she and her sister used to talk at length about everything that happened to them during the day. In fact, for several evenings after the funeral, she used to go to the cemetery west of town, which was located near their farm, and talk to the dirt on her sister's grave. This took Agatha back to the flu epidemic of 1918, when her dear brother Timothy had died. This was her first experience with death, and it left her, at the age of eight, mistrustful of God. She was amazed to discover herself speaking aloud of this to the three women around the table. She concluded, "You see, I kept expecting Tim to recover, and when he didn't, I blamed God."

And then just as Big Edna was about to tell her story, Agatha went on, recounting the other deaths of dear ones: her father and then, a year later, her mother, and Miles Pruitt, a teacher in the local public high school and her lodger for a number of years, who had been shot by a crazy woman, the mother of a student on their farm in the gulch west of town. And about ten years earlier she'd lost James O'Hannon, an Irish priest she'd been close to. And finally, most recently, within days of each other, two of her oldest friends had died, Lillian Kite and Thaddeus Druppers.

At this point she broke down and wept, realizing how intensely she missed Lillian. Wiping her eyes, she apologized to the others and said this would conclude the meeting. Big Edna objected—she hadn't yet had her turn—but Agatha wordlessly gathered up the papers and headed for the doorway.

"Miss McGee," Mrs. Severson called after her, "do we meet here again next Monday?"

Agatha stopped and turned, surprised that anyone would want to risk another meeting where its leader broke down and cried. She wanted to tell them that she had chaired the meeting by default and that she had no training in this work. Instead she asked, "Would you like to?"

"Of course," said Mrs. Severson and Harriet together. Big Edna said she'd bring cookies. The shawled woman didn't commit herself but sat there with a small smile playing across her lips.

Who is that woman? Agatha asked herself on her way back to her apartment, *and why does she intimidate me so?* She laid the papers on her kitchen table and went to the phone. She called her house and got Frederick on the line.

"Hi Agatha, how did it go?"

"What happened to you, Frederick?"

"Me? Oh, I came home."

"And why did you do that?"

"I guess I didn't care for the group all that much. You know, all women."

"But the group exists for your sake, don't you remember?"

"Yep, I remember."

"Well?"

"I just can't do it, Agatha. I'm real sorry, but I just can't say out loud all the stuff I want to say to a roomful of women. Especially those women. I mean Mrs. Hillyard is so fancy and Mrs. Bingham is—I don't know, so high and mighty or something. If I had known—"

"Mrs. Bingham! So that's who that is: Corrine Bingham!" Corrine Bingham, a difficult student to handle, had been in one of Agatha's first classes. She later married an Indian from the Sandhill Reservation and had two daughters, one of whom, Beverly, was now married to Mayor Mulholland. Before her marriage she'd been Beverly Bingham, the student whose welfare Miles Pruitt was looking after when her mother shot him dead in their farmyard. Agatha felt a wave of panic overtake her. "What's she doing on the loose?" she screeched into the phone. "I thought she'd been sentenced to life in the hospital for the criminally insane."

"I guess she's out on good behavior."

"In the sixth grade she was forever distracting the other pupils and she never did her homework." There was a hitch in her voice. "She murdered Miles Pruitt, for heaven's sake."

Frederick was silent on the line. He never knew what to say when Agatha got worked up.

When she finally got control of herself, she said, "Well, all right, Frederick. We're meeting once more next Monday. I'll expect you to show up."

Next, she phoned Judge Caferty and asked him how Mrs. Bingham could have been let loose in the community.

At first he didn't know whom she was talking about, so she gave him a detailed account of that awful day thirty-odd years ago. It was the day of the confrontation with the people from the Sandhill Reservation, she told him, and Governor Gunderson—the first Governor Gunderson—had posted the National Guard in the Bingham farmyard overnight. It became clear at the trial that the National Guard had driven Mrs. Bingham crazy by whooping it up all night and killing several of her chickens."

"Oh yes, I remember," said the judge.

"Wait a minute; let me finish. After the National Guard left in the morning, Mrs. Bingham stood with her rifle at an upstairs window, determined to shoot the next man who stepped foot on her property, and the next man was Miles Pruitt. Maynard, you remember him surely."

"Yes, I remember, Agatha. He was a teacher in Staggerford."

"At her trial, all she said was, 'They killed my chickens.' She repeated it over and over, and the only good that came out of it was that the commander of the National Guard was disciplined and Governor Gunderson, a Republican, was defeated at the next election."

When she had apparently finished speaking, the judge ventured to say, "That was Governor Gunderson senior."

"Yes, I just told you that. But I didn't call you to talk about Governor Gunderson, Maynard, I called to ask you what Mrs. Bingham is doing out in the world?"

"Well, Agatha, I can't rightly say, but I imagine she's out on parole. A lot of our prisoners were released recently because of the state's budget shortfall. You know, it costs thousands of dollars to keep a person incarcerated these days."

"Budget shortfall be damned. This woman is a murderer."

"It's true she killed a man, but the authorities, the parole board, must have considered her safe enough in her old age."

Agatha slammed down the phone, but seconds later it rang and she picked it up again. It was Judge Caferty saying, "Agatha, I've been meaning to ask you, could you come over on Sunday afternoon and play a little recital for a few guests I'm having in?"

Her reply was adamant. "How many times do I have to tell you? I don't play the piano anymore, Maynard, not for you or anybody else!"

As soon as she hung up on him the second time, she regretted being so harsh with him, but she couldn't seem to control the emotion—the anger—caused by Mrs. Bingham being back in circulation.

25

After a night of restless sleep, Agatha was standing at her stove soft-boiling an egg for breakfast when John Beezer turned up at her door.

"I ain't seen you lately, Missus."

"I *haven't* seen you lately—"

"That's 'cause I been out to Ernie's place, my old farm. Ernie and his new lady friend was steppin' out and I was what you call their babysitter. 'Cept the baby ain't no baby no more. You seen her, Missus, you know how big she is."

"The baby *isn't* a baby *any*more."

"That's what I just said." He raised his voice, assuming she'd suddenly turned hard of hearing. "She's got a mind of her own, that kid."

"Mr. Beezer, I am not repeating everything you say. I am correcting your grammar."

"Oh yeah, I forgot." He looked so ashamed that she softened her voice and asked if he'd like an egg for breakfast.

"Don't mind if I do," he said, taking a seat at her table.

She served him the boiled egg in an eggcup and put a fresh egg in the water. Waiting for it to boil, she recalled the day she moved into Sunset Senior for the second time and how she'd decided to bring along two of her four eggcups because they were the oldest things she owned. Her great-grandmother, her Grandfather Cunningham's mother, had brought them from England when she came to America in 1829.

John Beezer said, "I don't believe that kid was in bed before midnight any time I been out there. Why, she stays up watchin' TV till she drops off to sleep in her chair is what she does."

Agatha was pleased to see that instead of starting to eat, he was waiting for her to join him. She took this to be a sign of his intrinsic good manners.

Actually, he'd have tucked into his egg right away, but he'd never before encountered an eggcup and he didn't know what to do with it. When she finally took her place at the table, he watched closely as she broke off the top of her shell with her knife and dug her spoon down into the egg. It didn't look all that hard, so he picked up his knife, but in trying to lop off the top of his egg, he tipped it over, the egg landing on the table in front of him and the eggcup crashing to the floor and breaking into a hundred pieces.

"Dang, *dang*!" he said. "Now look what I gone and done."

"Don't worry about it," she said, stooping over and dropping the larger pieces into her wastebasket and then wetting a paper towel to pick up the tiny shards. "There've already been two broken out of what began as a set of six. My Great-grandmother Cunningham broke one on her journey to America almost a hundred and seventy years ago, and Lillian Kite broke the second one as she was drying dishes last summer." She'd told Lillian the same thing, "Don't worry about it," but after Lillian had gone home, she'd cried, picturing her dear Grandfather Cunningham eating out of the eggcup his whole life and her mother doing the same. She thought it odd that she didn't feel like crying now.

She shelled his egg and put it in a bowl for him, and when he'd finished eating, she said, "You will have to excuse me now, Mr. Beezer; I am going to see the priest."

He rose quickly from his chair and gave her a little bow, saying, "Let me know how much that thingamajig, that funny little egg dish, sets you back and I'll pay you for it."

"Never mind," she told him. "There was a time in my life when that eggcup meant a great deal to me but not anymore."

For several minutes, getting ready to visit the parish house, she puzzled over this statement, wondering why it was true.

It was a balmy morning for early February. Under the snowbanks, runnels of melting snow were audibly flowing into the gutters. She heard chickadees and redpolls chirping as if it were spring, and she thought she saw—although she couldn't be sure—a robin sitting high in a big oak tree.

At the rectory, she rapped on the door and Father Healy let her in. "Ah, Miss McGee, I'm very happy to see you."

"Why should you be happy? I always come to you with problems."

"Because of your lively mind. Don't laugh; I've just spent several days with Leonard Fossum. By the way, he fixed the doorbell." He reached around the doorjamb and pressed the button. It set off a jangle somewhere at the back of the house. "He's a fine handyman, but terribly tiresome." He switched off the television and asked her to please sit down.

He plopped onto the couch and she took a straight chair facing him, saying, "I have come to you for two reasons, Father. First to say how sorry I am to hear about your illness."

"My illness?" He looked puzzled.

"Your cancer."

"Oh, that. It was nothing. I had a growth removed from my back that turned out to be benign. My, news does travel fast around here."

"Indeed it does. My grandnephew Frederick told me about it the night before last. Can you be sure there's no malignancy?"

"Oh yes, the doctor is quite positive about it."

"Well then, I'll move on to my second reason for coming to see you. It's a moral problem, Father. I find myself—could it be?—hating someone." She told him about Mrs. Bingham and her support group.

He didn't smile or laugh, which pleased her, and she went on to say that if the person showed up again next week, she didn't see how she could carry on.

He looked away, as if he were studying something far off. Finally he said, "I'm sorry, but I have had no experience with hatred."

"No, I don't expect you have." She believed him. He was such an easygoing man he'd probably never in his life truly despised anyone. "I haven't come here to find out whether you've ever felt the way I do. I've come to ask what I must do about it."

"Well . . . you remember what Jesus said about our enemies?"

"Yes, we are to love them. I was afraid you were going to say that. Because how can I love somebody who murdered my friend Miles?"

"It's not easy, of course, but you've experienced forgiving an enemy."

"I have?"

"Yes, Imogene Kite, your friend Lillian's daughter. You voted for her to become our librarian."

"Who told you that?"

"Lillian told me. She said Imogene had done you a great wrong and you voted for her anyway."

Agatha was surprised and pleased to think that Lillian had remembered this generous act. She'd never spoken about it to Agatha. "But at least Imogene wasn't a murderer, Father."

"No, you're right, of course, but she destroyed your reputation, and that's pretty serious."

Agatha nodded, thinking back several years to her trip to Italy. While she was gone, Frederick had let Imogene into her house and she had gone to work like a ferret, finding a number of Agatha's old letters and reading them and spreading her private opinions around town. Despite this, Agatha, as a member of the library board, cast the deciding vote for Imogene as director of the local Carnegie library.

"What I suggest you do, Miss McGee, is perform some act of kindness toward Mrs. Bingham, and let me know what comes of it, if anything."

She sat silent for a moment, considering this advice. If kindness was what her pastor recommended, of course she'd do it, but it wouldn't be easy.

"I'll be interested to hear how it turns out," he said, and added, "Now how about a cup of tea?"

"No, thanks," she said rising from her chair. "I have to get to work on my plans for the meeting of the group I'm leading next Monday."

It was typical of Agatha that although there were six days between now and the next meeting, she would go to work immediately. As a classroom teacher she had devoted the first day of every vacation to lesson plans even if her next class wouldn't meet for two weeks, or even three months. Today, jotting down notes at her kitchen table, she was surprised at how engrossed she became, how eagerly she was anticipating the support group. She decided to open the evening, for the benefit of Mrs. Severson, with a description of her own reaction to the death of loved ones, as she had previously. It always helped to know that others had suffered what you were suffering. She stood up and paced her apartment, composing the lecture in her head, recalling her meek acceptance of the deaths of her beloved parents and her outrage at the death of Miles Pruitt a few years later. More recently, the death of her dear friend Lillian had caused her to feel defiant and angry at God. (She had consulted Father

Healy about this and he'd told her, "Don't worry about it, Miss McGee. God is big; God can take it.")

After that she would open it up for discussion. The group would speak of their own experiences with death. She was sure that most of them were mature enough to handle this topic with aplomb, but, of course, there was no telling what was going on in Mrs. Bingham's clouded mind. Also, it was hard to gauge how long this discussion would last. She remembered her sixth graders and how some days they wouldn't stop talking and on other days they had hardly anything to say. They seemed prompted by some force outside themselves, something like the weather. In fact, Agatha had developed the theory over the years that classroom behavior depended on high or low pressure in the atmosphere. On cloudy days of low pressure, her students were restless and talkative and some even misbehaved and needed disciplining, while on bright days of high pressure she noticed they were usually listless and silent. To test her theory, she had hung a barometer next to her door and consulted it each day on her way to work. Her theory proved fairly correct, but it wasn't foolproof. It was wrong approximately one day out of four.

Next, she would have them write an essay entitled *What I Wish*. This was a device Miles Pruitt used to spring on his high school students and the resulting essays were so revealing that Agatha felt guilty about reading the ones he showed her— despite Miles's claim that his students had greatly benefited from the assignment because they got a lot of heavy stuff off their chests.

And, finally, she would ask the group to write brief evaluations of the support group, telling her whether they wished to continue or drop it.

By noon she was finished with her preparations. After lunch in the dining room she went to her rocking chair and dozed in the sun, wishing the support group would meet that night instead of the next Monday. Each day for the rest of the week she tried to think of a kindness she could do for Mrs. Bingham, but she had no luck.

Each evening she checked the weather show, and on the following Sunday she found that the barometric pressure was ideal for good behavior.

26

On Monday evening on her way down the hallway, Agatha heard a lot of loud conversation emanating from the dining room and she wondered if Little Edna had scheduled another meeting of some kind. She had failed to tell Little Edna that her group was meeting again tonight.

And, sure enough, sitting at the dining room tables were at least a dozen people, most of them strangers to Agatha, with Little Edna and Joe sitting front and center. Everyone fell silent and stared at Agatha. She spotted Mrs. Severson and Mrs. Bingham and said to them, "I'm very sorry for the mix-up; my group will meet in my apartment this evening. If you will please follow me."

Voices of objection arose, and Agatha leaned over to hear Little Edna say, "This *is* your group, Miss McGee."

"My group? But there were to be only four."

"It seems word got out. I take it that many are your former students. Joe and I are just dropping in for fun."

Her husband nodded pleasantly, affirming this.

"Tonight will hardly be fun," said Agatha. "The subject is death." She raised her voice. "I am Miss McGee, formerly a teacher at St. Isidore's. I started what we call this support group last week, and I am surprised to see so many of you here this evening."

She saw John Beezer sitting near Harriet. Mrs. Teague was there, and Big Edna was back for more. She didn't see Frederick.

"I hope you all aren't seeking relief from mental illness, because I am strictly an amateur in this field. The subject tonight is *death,* a gloomy topic certainly, and if you would like to leave now, you are welcome to do so, because it is most impolite to get up and walk out while someone is speaking."

She paused, looking at her notes, but no one left.

"All right," she said. "When I finish we will have a discussion, at which time we will introduce ourselves."

Her account of her own reaction to death took only fifteen minutes. She concluded with Father Healy's advice to her concerning her anger at God. "He said to me, 'Relax, Miss McGee. God is big; God can take it.' Well, I have pondered those words long and hard, and I don't know what to make of them. I mean, suppose he's right? I would truly love to think that it makes no difference to God how mad I get at funerals." She paused, and decided this would be a good place to stop. "And now I would like to hear your thoughts on this subject. You will begin by saying your name and why you are here."

She pointed to a bright-looking woman sitting in the front row who said, "My name is Bernice Falk. I used to be Bernice Dodson, Miss McGee. I went through the sixth grade under you, and now that my kids are reared and out of the house, I've decided I want to feel like a sixth grader again." She described the recent death from cancer of her husband's father, George Falk, a hardware merchant in Berrington, and while she spoke, Agatha recalled the twelve-year-old Bernice Dodson sitting primly in the front row of her classroom, one of the most obedient students she'd ever had. Whenever Agatha read aloud to the class, Bernice invariably sat with her hands folded on her desk the way Agatha had to keep reminding her other students to sit. And she was still doing Agatha's bidding, judging by her use of the word *reared.* Agatha remembered insisting that *reared* was the proper word for bringing up children, not *raised.* She resisted the urge to ask Bernice why she wanted to feel like a sixth grader again—that would have sidetracked the discussion. When Bernice had finished speaking, Agatha pointed to a plain-looking woman with long gray hair who looked familiar.

This was Nadine Oppegard, who had been a student of Agatha's thirty years earlier. "I'm visiting my parents, who are both in the Staggerford Care Center. My dad had a heart attack, so I took some time off from my job teaching art history in Massachusetts. I'm like you, Miss McGee—if he dies, I'm going to be mighty pissed. Surely you remember him."

Agatha cringed at the vulgarity, but let it pass. Nadine would soon take her long gray hair back to Massachusetts, leaving Staggerford pristine once again. She said, "Of course I remember him. For many years Dr. Oppegard was the only dentist in town." Meeting him on the street—a small, pale, wizened man—she used to wonder how someone so weak looking had the strength to pull teeth.

Most of the people in the group turned out not to be strangers. Four more, like Bernice and Nadine, had been students of Agatha's at one time or another, and hearing about the support group, they had come to renew a relationship that had once been of great value to them. Two of them she didn't remember, but she could picture all six names in her grade book:

Ashcraft
Becker
Dodson
Northrup
Oppegard
White

The last of these, Sylvia White Hoffman, had just begun to speak when Mrs. Bingham blurted, "How much longer do we have to listen to this crap? My ass is gettin' mighty tired."

Agatha suddenly felt so exhausted that she couldn't utter a

word of reprimand. The rest of the group shushed Mrs. Bingham and then turned back to Agatha, who was sinking onto a folding chair. She realized that she'd been standing for more than three quarters of an hour without feeling the least bit tired. Another principle she'd carried away from the classroom, besides her barometric theory, was that a good class always fed energy into the teacher, while a difficult class took energy away.

She lowered her head and closed her eyes, trying to gather strength enough to dismiss the group. When she opened them again, Little Edna was heading to the freezer behind the serving counter and saying, "It's time for a break, everybody. You can have your ice cream in a cone or a bowl, whichever you prefer." Big Edna said, "I've baked cookies, but I'm not sure I've brought enough."

While everyone else milled about, visiting with each other and eating ice cream and cookies, Bernice Dodson and Mrs. Severson pulled chairs up beside Agatha and expressed concern about her health. "You turned pale all of a sudden," said Bernice.

Agatha shook her head despairingly, telling herself she was too old to be leading a support group. If only the social worker from Berrington had been here to take over.

"Yes, you did," said Mrs. Severson. "But you look a lot better now." She asked Bernice, "Doesn't she look better?"

"Yes," said Bernice, "it's obvious in your face." She put an arm around her old teacher's shoulders, which felt so good it made Agatha want to cry.

She drew a hankie from her sleeve and wiped her eyes. Holding back her tears, she said, "Thank you both."

Sylvia White, a willowy blonde wearing thick glasses, soon joined them, as did Nadine Oppegard, making a circle of five. Agatha introduced everyone, and the younger ones were shocked to learn that Mrs. Severson had been Agatha's student as long ago as 1933. "But Miss McGee," said Sylvia White, "you don't look a day older than you did when I left the sixth grade."

"You must have been born around 1910 to be teaching school by 1933," said Bernice boldly.

"Precisely," said Agatha. Her attention was drawn to Mrs. Bingham, who was leaving the room. As soon as she was out of sight, Agatha felt better.

"It's 1998," said Bernice, "so you're eighty-eight. My goodness, you're doing marvelously."

"I'm eighty-seven. My birthday isn't until September," said Agatha, her gaze lingering on the doorway through which Mrs. Bingham had disappeared.

Seeing this, Mrs. Severson asked, "Who was that woman?"

"Corrine Bingham, a dangerous person," said Agatha. She had to raise her voice because the chatter in the room was growing louder. "She's been in prison for murder."

"Not Beverly Bingham's mother?" asked Nadine Oppegard.

"The same. That's right, Nadine, you were in high school about that time."

"I was a classmate of Beverly's." As Nadine told the others about the death of her English teacher, Catherine Northrup, a short, dark-haired woman wearing a kind of jumpsuit Agatha had never seen before, joined the group. She asked Nadine to start over from the beginning, which she did.

Agatha turned away, not wishing to relive that horrible day when Miles Pruitt died, and saw John Beezer hurry out of the dining room. Taking this as a sign that the meeting was breaking up, she stood up and said, "Well, ladies, I guess that concludes our business. It's wonderful to see you again, all of you."

"Hey, not so fast," said Bernice. "We haven't finished our stories about death."

She saw that the people left in the room, having fallen silent when she stood up, were taking their seats again.

"I'm sorry." Agatha addressed Mrs. Severson because, being the closest to her in age, she'd certainly understand. "It appears eighty-seven is too old to be leading discussions."

"Don't worry about that," said Bernice, turning Agatha's chair so that it faced front. "You just sit here and listen and we'll lead the discussion."

Agatha did as she was told. She resented losing control of the evening but was too exhausted to object. Besides, the recital of grief was interesting. She heard Addie Greeno tell of the death of her husband during the second year of their marriage. He'd been accidentally shot by another hunter during deer season. Upon hearing he was dead, Addie said, she'd turned numb and remained numb for a year. "I don't remember a thing from that year. It was like being in a coma. I didn't come back to reality until the phone rang one day the next summer and it was old Father O'Connor asking if I'd come and cook a meal at the parish house because he was having guests in. So that was the beginning of my career as housekeeper for Staggerford's priests. I did that for thirty-some years until the current priest, Father Healy, moved to town. Father Healy doesn't have a housekeeper and you can see it in the way he eats. I'll just bet that if he'd been eating right over the years, he wouldn't be dying of cancer today."

Agatha made a mental note to correct Addie tomorrow, when her strength returned, concerning the state of Father Healy's health. And what was Addie doing here in the first place? Bernice had failed to ask the speakers why they'd come.

The final speaker of the evening was Big Edna, who said that she, too, had lost her husband early in their marriage. They'd been married exactly three years and twenty-two days when Ben was killed in a car accident. When she heard the news, she reacted two different ways. "I felt numb the way Addie did, and I started in to eat. I was normal sized before Ben died and I've been heavy ever since. I know what a fool I look like to everybody. When you meet me for the first time, I know what goes through your head. You say to yourself, 'I wonder what that woman weighs.' Well, you don't need to wonder anymore because I'll tell you what I weigh. Yesterday on the drugstore scale I weighed right around two hundred and fifty pounds."

Before Agatha could interject a word, Bernice Dodson concluded the meeting by saying, "All right, everybody, we'll see you here next Monday; tell your friends." Then Bernice and Catherine Northrup took her by the arms, unnecessarily, and accompanied her down the hallway to her room. On the way Agatha asked, "How did you girls find out about tonight's meeting?"

"We read it in the paper," said Catherine Northrup.

"What paper? Surely not the *Weekly*."

Bernice nodded, quoting the notice, "Support group led by Miss Agatha McGee. Come to Sunset Senior Apartments to relieve your stress."

"Oh no, who put that in? I had an idea that tonight's meeting would be the last." Actually, this idea hadn't crossed her mind until this evening's outburst by Mrs. Bingham.

"No, no," said Bernice, "we're just getting started."

"Yes, please, Miss McGee, for the sake of your former students. There'll be even more of us next week, I'm sure." Agatha's heart was warmed by the thought of her former students coming to see her, and she relented. "All right," she said, "we'll try it once more next week and see if Mrs. Bingham can keep silent."

When they left, Agatha went directly to her rocking chair and picked her copy of the *Staggerford Weekly* off the coffee table. Sure enough, there on page three, under "Community Events," was the announcement. She phoned the publisher, Lee Fremling, at home and asked him, "Who put the announcement in your paper about a support group meeting?"

"Huh?" Fremling responded.

She repeated her question.

"Who wants to know?" he asked.

"This is Agatha McGee."

"Oh, Miss McGee." He sounded like someone coming to attention for although he had never been a student of hers, he, like the rest of Staggerford, had learned to stand up a little straighter in Agatha's presence. "Sorry, I didn't catch your question."

She asked for a third time.

"I can find out for you tomorrow at the earliest. I can call you in the morning."

"That will be fine. Call me at ten."

Next, she phoned Frederick and asked where he'd been during the evening.

"Takin' a nap," he said.

"Frederick, there's nothing wrong with your memory. I shouldn't have had to call to remind you about the meeting."

"No, you're right; I remembered. I just didn't come."

"But you are the reason the group exists."

"I know it. I feel bad about it."

Agatha felt bad too, felt betrayed, in fact—and for the first time ever, by Frederick. "All right, tell me why."

"I told you, Agatha, how I can't tell my troubles to that bunch of women."

"There were two men there tonight."

"I found somebody to talk to about my problems."

"Who?"

"A guy on my route. Albert Goltz." Twice the previous week and again that day, Mr. Goltz had been waiting at his mailbox when Frederick came by on his route, and invited him in for coffee. They traded war stories and love stories. Goltz, who had been jilted as a young man and never married, seemed as eager for these sessions as Frederick.

"Goltz," said Agatha. "I don't believe I know anybody by that name."

"That's right; he says he's never met you."

"Well, is he helping you?"

"Yep, or I'm helping myself by talking about things. It's like you said, Agatha—talking helps. And Goltz is a good listener."

"Perhaps he'd come and speak to my Monday night group."

"No, I'm afraid not. He's pretty shy."

"A shy psychologist."

"He's not a psychologist. He's more of a gardener, I'd say. He's got this huge flower garden next to his house."

Anyone with a huge garden couldn't be all bad, thought Agatha, who was very fond of flowers. She wrote the name *Goltz* on a piece of notepaper along with the phone number of the president of the Staggerford Garden Club, to which she used to belong. The club was always on the lookout for successful gardeners as speakers at their monthly meetings. She'd call the president in the morning.

"All right, Frederick, I'll let you go if you're sure you'll be all right."

"I'll make it," he mumbled, and they said good-bye.

It was nearly ten o'clock, but she wasn't ready for bed. The overall effect of tonight's meeting, despite Mrs. Bingham, had been to energize her. She rocked in her chair and thought about flowers. She pictured a whole garden full of daisies, her favorite blossom. She couldn't wait for spring and the flower bed John Beezer promised to put in front of the apartments. She must ask him to include daisies in the mix. Was John Beezer aware that there was a Staggerford Men's Garden Club as well? He might enjoy attending their meetings. She phoned his apartment to tell him. After four rings a distinctively deep woman's voice answered. Mrs. Bingham's voice. Agatha said, "Wrong number," and hung up.

27

Early the next morning, after a night of wakefulness and nightmares, Agatha was about to go to Little Edna's apartment to ask if she knew that Mrs. Bingham had been in John Beezer's rooms last night, but then she realized that Little Edna wouldn't understand her motives. She'd assume that Agatha was a prudish gossip, when actually she was worried about John Beezer's getting mixed up with the crazy woman. Agatha didn't feel up to explaining, going over the story of Miles's death once again, so she sat fuming over her breakfast of waffles and syrup. No matter the state of her emotions, Agatha's appetite hardly ever failed her.

Later, sitting in her rocking chair sipping tea and thinking fondly of the six former students who'd come to last night's meeting, she saw what looked like a small moving van backing between the cars in the parking lot and up to the back door of the apartments. Because she knew of no empty rooms in the building, she assumed the driver was lost, and she went to work on her plans for next week's meeting.

She hadn't gotten to the *What I Wish* papers the night before and she probably wouldn't again the following week, everybody being such a ready talker, so she'd have them up her sleeve in case time began to drag. Next week she would lighten up. Having taken care of death, she would lead a discussion about lifelong friends. That way, she might be able to put Lillian's death behind her. She would tell stories about her girlhood with Lillian and about their adult years. And then, if an even larger group of her former students materialized, as Bernice Dodson had predicted, she would hear about more of the young women who had passed through her classroom and maybe even some of the young men. In magazines and newspapers Agatha was especially fond of "What's-Become-of-So-and-So" articles. The trouble with teaching as a career was that you never knew what became of most of the people you had a hand in forming. You spent your life shaping the minds and the moral sense of countless youngsters, and unless they stayed around town as adults, which very few of them did, you never heard of them again.

This thought was interrupted by the telephone—Addie asking if she deserved an A for her account last night of her husband's death.

Agatha had to smile, realizing that some people still carried around the image of her as a sixth grade teacher. She said, "Yes, of course, Addie. It was quite touching; I was moved."

Addie said, "Good," and hung up.

At precisely ten o'clock, Agatha's phone rang again, and she assumed it was Lee Fremling getting back to her. "Hello," she said without asking for the caller's identity, "and thank you for calling back so promptly."

But it wasn't Lee Fremling. It was Father Healy saying, "No trouble at all, Miss McGee. I just thought I'd call to ask how you made out with the troublemaker last night."

"Not well at all, Father. She left early and I didn't get a chance to do her a kindness."

"There's no hurry; I just thought I'd check."

"Though the Lord only knows what I'll do for her. I've been wracking my brain trying to figure it out."

"Relax, Miss McGee. Sooner or later the opportunity will present itself, and you'll know."

"Oh, I have my doubts about that, Father, but I'll try to take your word for it."

"And how was the rest of your support group last night?"

"It was fine. Father, I have to ask you a question."

"Yes?"

"Do you follow up with all of your parishioners by phone like this?"

He laughed, "No, I don't. It's just that your relationship with that woman is so interesting that I had to ask."

She signed off without telling him, for fear he'd swell with pride (a venial sin), how much she appreciated being taken seriously. She realized at that moment that that was what had been missing from her life: she hadn't been taken seriously since retiring from teaching more than fifteen years ago. That was why she had become so instantly fond of Harriet. The woman respected her. In fact, that was why she had been feeling more positive these last few weeks: she had been warmed by the respect of nearly everyone she'd met, not least of all John Beezer and the Rinkwitzes. And now even Addie Greeno, who all her life had been imperious in Agatha's presence, revealed that Agatha's opinion meant a great deal to her. Siting in her big old house on River Street, she had let the world pass her by, had seen very few people, had forgotten what a healthy harvest of serious respect she used to gather up wherever she went in Staggerford.

Her phone rang again. She said, "I'm sorry the line was busy when you called earlier, Mr. Fremling."

But again, it wasn't Lee Fremling. It was a woman's voice, Big Edna's. "How about my description last night of how Ben died, Agatha? Did it meet with your approval?" she asked.

"Yes, of course it did. Why do you ask?"

"Because Addie got an A on hers, and I wondered how mine compared."

Agatha sat up a little straighter in her rocker—her posture during her teaching years—and said, "It was the equal of Addie's. And while I'm at it, I might as well say how moved I was to think you went through all that suffering . . ." She stopped short of saying it changed her opinion of Big Edna for that would be admitting that she hadn't previously held a high opinion of her. It crossed her mind that another principle of teaching applied to Big Edna and Addie Greeno, that the more you learned about a person, the better you liked her, or at least you had more sympathy for her.

"I have a piece of news for you," said Big Edna, rewarding Agatha for her A. "You know that heavyset woman who disrupted last night's meeting? Well, she's moving into Sunset Senior this morning. And not only that, she's moving into John Beezer's apartment."

Agatha hung up the phone and went to her door. Squinting down the hallway, she saw Clement Crumley, the drayman, leaning on the outside of John Beezer's doorjamb and conversing with somebody in the apartment. This was a matter for the manager, so she went to see the Rinkwitzes.

Trying to keep emotion out of her voice, she said to Little Edna, "I'm told Corrine Bingham is moving into John Beezer's rooms."

"That's right," said Edna, drying dishes in her kitchen, not appearing the least upset.

"But she's been in the hospital for the criminally insane. What about your waiting list?"

"Oh, she's been on our waiting list for months. Her probation officer called and arranged it last fall, before they let her out of prison. He asked me to have a room for her around the first of February. Well, as you know, nothing has opened up since Calvin Christianson moved in, so she's spent the last two weeks living in a motel, which wasn't the best situation, according to the parole office. He kept pressing me for an apartment, and finally her brother agreed to double up until a place opens up for her."

"John Beezer is her brother?"

"Yes, she's a Beezer from Bartlett."

Then it dawned on Agatha that Corrine Bingham had been, as a girl, a Beezer.

"The state of Minnesota has bought her a single bed and we've curtained off part of John's living room, where she'll sleep."

"If you're concerned about what she said at last night's meeting," Little Edna continued, "her parole officer told me that most prisoners feel unstable until they get settled down. He says she's harmless and she'll be fine. Incidentally, you had a very nice turnout last night, didn't you?"

"Yes, somebody put it in the paper and it attracted quite a crowd."

"That was me. I put it in the paper because I knew there were people in the area who wanted to see you again. Besides, it's good for Staggerfordians to see our operation here. A lot of them think of this as a regular old folks' home."

"So I was used as a public relations ploy."

Having caught the edge in Agatha's voice, she looked sharply at her, asking, "Do you object, Miss McGee?"

Agatha answered obliquely, "Well, I can hardly complain because it worked out to my benefit."

Little Edna excused herself to answer a knock on her door. It was Janet Meers asking for Agatha. When she saw Agatha in the room, she brushed past Edna and came in and embraced her. Janet was Agatha's friend who'd been in Florida with her husband, the Realtor.

"Janet, what are you doing back in the North? Winter isn't over."

"Well, the person who ran our Staggerford office up and quit suddenly, so I came back to run things until Randy hires another office manager. I spent last night at a motel and I've just been out to the house to get the water and heat up and running. I thought I'd come and see you while the place is warming up. How are you, Agatha?"

"Not bad. I've started a support group for Frederick, which Frederick refuses to attend."

"I guess that was predictable. Frederick is awfully private about his feelings."

"But he's so unhappy, Janet. Your sister Lee Ann left him, and it breaks my heart to see him moping."

"You know, Agatha, I've decided some people are simply not meant to be happy."

They left the managers' apartment and strolled down the hallway together.

"Randy, for example," she continued, speaking of her husband. "I don't believe Randy has ever spent an entire happy day in his life. Real estate is the only thing that seems to satisfy him. He loves showing properties to potential buyers. But once the sale is complete, he always finds something to fret about. We went on a cruise while we were in Florida—you know, a five-day jaunt around the Caribbean islands. We both agreed that a few days away would do us good, but Randy worried the whole time. He worries about the business and he worries about our kids."

"How are they, Janet?" Both Janet's son and daughter, now in their twenties, were Agatha's godchildren.

"They're fine. Stephen and his new wife live in Madison, where he teaches high school manual training—he calls it shop—and Sara is off doing charity work in Guatemala. Of course, it's Sara he worries about most these days. He's afraid she'll be attacked by wild animals or wild natives. But my point is, there's an aspect of Frederick that reminds me of Randy. It's as if both of them lack the capacity for happiness."

Agatha considered this idea but rejected it. "No, Janet," she said, "I can't believe anybody is denied happiness by the wrong set of genes. Frederick claims, in fact, that he's coming out of the doldrums since we started the group."

"But you said he doesn't attend."

"He doesn't. He talks his troubles out to somebody else, a friend on his mail route, a man named Goltz. You see, he wouldn't have broken the ice with Mr. Goltz if I hadn't had the idea for a support group. And by the way, you must attend next time, Janet, because a number of my former students will be there. Catherine Northrup was there last time. You knew her, didn't you?"

"Sure, she was a year ahead of me." It turned out that Janet was acquainted with three of the six former students at the last meeting. She said she would love to attend the next week.

"Step in and see my apartment," said Agatha surprising herself. Time was when she'd felt very self-conscious about the smallness of her new place and she'd never allow any friend from the outside in to see it.

"This will take some getting used to," said Janet, standing between the kitchenette and the sitting room, "thinking of you here, after a lifetime in your house." She pointed to the doorway near the TV. "Your bedroom's in there, I suppose."

"Yes, and the bathroom beyond. Come and see." Then reading Janet's expression of disappointment, she said, "You don't like it."

"No, no, I like it fine." Janet resisted adding *But not for you.* "It's just that I've been thinking of you in your house all these years, so I'll have to change my image of you."

"Not your image of me, Janet. Your image of where I live. My space is diminished, but I'm not." She didn't mention that it had taken months for her to reach this level of confidence.

Janet sat down and visited over a cup of tea, then embraced her once again and left. In the hallway she was approached by an elderly man and woman she didn't know. The woman glowered at her, while the man, wearing an altogether more congenial expression, asked, "Is the new woman in there?"

"I beg your pardon?" said Janet.

"Missus McGee, is she home?"

"Yes," Janet said.

Before stepping outside, Janet turned and gazed at the two of them standing at Agatha's door. They were so curious looking, particularly the woman. So shapeless. So unkempt. And she seemed so antagonistic.

Agatha, when she saw Mrs. Bingham standing behind him, regretted inviting John Beezer into the apartment. They sat at the kitchen table. Mrs. Bingham scowled at Agatha's midsection while John said, "I was tellin' my sister here about your lessons and she says she could use a little brushup herself."

"Lessons?" said Agatha, standing at her stove, boiling water for more tea. "Last night's session was hardly what you'd call lessons."

"No, I mean *my* lessons. How to talk and such. You know, how not to say ain't."

Agatha knew what was coming and was horrified at the thought of having to communicate with this awful woman.

"So, I was wondering if you'd take my sister here and polish her up the way you done me. You see, all the women in this place are pretty high-toned and she says she hates 'em all. But I tell her it makes more sense that if you can't lick 'em, join 'em."

Agatha said, "The first thing she'd have to do is stop the outbursts like last night's at the meeting of our group. That sort of thing will turn everybody against her."

"Yeah, I already told her that. I says, 'Corrine, you ain't gonna get very far' "—he corrected himself—"I mean, 'You *aren't* gonna get very far talkin' like that around here.' " Whereas everyone else, including Agatha, pronounced her name Cor-IN, her brother said Cor-EEN.

Agatha would remember this conversation for the rest of her days. She thought it marked a turning point in her life. She knew she could not turn down this request. This was what Father

Healy had spoken of. He'd said the opportunity to do a kindness to Mrs. Bingham would present itself, and Agatha had promised to seize it.

"I will do it," she said to John Beezer, and he looked very pleased.

She set the teapot and three cups on the table and sat down. Both visitors stared at her over their steaming drinks. Agatha risked a glance at Mrs. Bingham and saw her usual forbidding expression. Her brother had his eyebrows raised in expectation, evidently waiting for Agatha to begin today's lesson.

She said, "Well, I can't start until she says something, Mr. Beezer."

"Oh, she'll talk all right. Once you get her started, she'll talk a leg off you."

"And how do we get her started?"

"Just ask her a question, same as you done me."

Agatha was puzzled. "I asked you a question?"

"Sure thing. You asked me where I come from."

"Oh, so I did."

" 'Cept for Old Man Druppers, you was the first person to talk to me in this place."

She felt a surge of pity for the man. Pity being a feeling she did not trust, she quickly put it out of her mind and said, "You were, not you was."

John Beezer bowed his head and repeated softly, "You were, you were."

They didn't stay long. After various comments about the weather—what past Februarys had been like, his predictions about future winters—John Beezer and his sister left, she without having uttered a single word. It's not a bad thing if she's cowed, thought Agatha; at least she'll keep quiet at next Monday's meeting.

28

At lunch Agatha had her first opportunity to correct Mrs. Bingham's language. Little Edna had announced that Imogene Kite, from the public library, was coming to Sunset Senior at two o'clock that afternoon to read to whichever residents were interested, and Mrs. Bingham, sitting across from Agatha, muttered to her brother, "I ain't interested."

"I'm *not* interested," Agatha had said, glancing up from her plate of biscuits and gravy. She saw that Mrs. Bingham was not as willing a student as her brother for she shot Agatha a hateful, angry scowl.

It was a look that lingered in Agatha's mind throughout the afternoon, and so she phoned Judge Caferty again and asked why Mrs. Bingham had been let out of the St. Peter Hospital for the Criminally Insane. He promised to get back to her with the answer.

At dinner on Wednesday evening she corrected her again when she heard Mrs. Bingham say to nobody in particular, "I hate lima beans." She told her, "*Hate* is too strong a word for what you mean. Here at Sunset Senior we might dislike something, but we don't hate it." Again the forbidding look.

On Thursday morning Judge Caferty called. He said it had been decided that Mrs. Bingham was not a danger to herself or the public anymore. "She's nearly eighty years old and going blind, and they need more room at the hospital for the criminal mental cases, so they let her out on parole."

"Going blind?" said Agatha. "She's no more blind than I am."

"That's what I was told," said the judge. "And by the way, yesterday I also learned that the woman from Bartlett isn't going to bring charges against her husband for taking their little girl, so you're off the hook, Agatha."

It took her a moment to understand what he was talking about, and by the time she did, he had already signed off. What good news this was. Although Mrs. Bingham had made her forget about the kidnapping, there was part of her brain that had been steadily and unconsciously fretting about it. She felt greatly relieved—buoyant in fact—to have this burden lifted from her. Energized by the development, she made it her single-minded mission to go after Mrs. Bingham's flaws.

At lunch, standing in line at the serving table, Mrs. Bingham said to Harriet, standing ahead of her, "I never know what fork to use. I don't cotton to all this silverware."

Agatha, behind her in line, said, "I believe *cotton,* when it's used in that way, is substandard English, Mrs. Bingham. Instead, you might say that you don't care for all this silverware, or you don't understand it, but not that you don't cotton to it." She steeled herself for the malevolent look, but this time the woman turned only halfway around to Agatha with a thoughtful look on her face, as if pondering the advice, said nothing, and then continued talking to Harriet.

Agatha knew her interruptions were paying off when, at Friday coffee, she heard Mrs. Bingham reply to Big Edna's comment about the weather by saying, "Yep, I ain—" and then, with a momentary glance at Agatha, she changed course. "Yep, I haven't seen February weather like this since 1984." She turned to her brother, saying, "Remember, Johnny? 'Eighty-four was the year you was visitin' Dad in the hospital ever' day and you said how nice it was right up to the funeral."

Agatha let the "you was" and the "ever' day" pass because she didn't want to break in on the fascinating story she was telling Big Edna. "On the day of the funeral—it was the second of March—a blizzard blew in. It thawed practically the whole month of February, then it snowed and the wind blew like crazy and only a handful of people got to the church. Leastways that's what Johnny told me, that only the Heiers from the next farm over from ours, and the Adamsons from down the road, got through the snow. At least the preacher made short work of the service, huh, Johnny?"

"Yeah," her brother replied, "it was real scary settin' there. The church was creakin' in the wind like it was goin' to blow away, and you'd look out and the snow was piling up in drifts, up to the windowsills on the south side."

His sister took over again. "I guess the trip to the cemetery was a god-awful mess. Cars stuck in the snow and blockin' the streets so the hearse had to turn around and take the body back to the mortuary and try it again the next day."

"The undertaker put chains on the hearse," John Beezer explained. "So he woulda made it if he coulda got through the stuck cars."

" 'Course, the weather didn't make a dang bit of difference to me where I was," said his sister. She paused with a pensive look on her face and then said, "You know, it comes to me now, talkin' about it, that bein' in St. Peter is like bein' dead, because if you're dead or if you're in St. Peter where I was, the weather don't make a dang bit of difference to you. 'Cept when they want you to go outside and get some exercise. That's always a bummer."

With the pen she always carried in a pocket, Agatha was jotting down on a paper napkin Mrs. Bingham's several mistakes

as they occurred. Then she turned to John Beezer, sitting on
her left, who had begun to thank her for all she was doing for his
sister.

"It's little enough to do, Mr. Beezer." She lowered her voice.
"But let me ask you about a rumor I've heard, that your sister is
going blind."

"That ain't no rumor, Missus, that's a fact."

"That *isn't* a rumor," she corrected.

"You got that right," he said.

Agatha discovered Mrs. Bingham to be an even quicker
study than her brother. Listening to her conversation with Big
Edna Brink across the table, Agatha heard her make not one
mistake of the sort she'd warned her about. And who had
worked on her table manners? During her first meals at Sunset
Senior she had leaned far over her food, as John Beezer used to
do, keeping her left arm curled around her plate. Now she sat
up straight. Agatha thought that except for her outmoded
clothes, particularly her worn-out, ever-present shawl, her unkempt hair, and the fierce scowl she was directing at everyone
again today, she was behaving just like her fellow residents. *At
this rate,* thought Agatha, *perhaps I won't have anything to fear
from Mrs. Bingham come Monday evening.*

Near the end of coffee hour, John Beezer's son Ernie turned
up with Jennie and Lee Ann Raft. Ernie nodded at Mrs. Bingham, mumbling her name, "Aunt Corrine," and pulled up a
chair next to his father and they talked about the price of hay
and milk. Agatha was quite sure that Lee Ann was avoiding her
for she stood at another table visiting with Mrs. Teague, whom
she was evidently acquainted with, then finally followed Jennie
over to Agatha's table. Jennie was fussed over by Mrs. Bingham.
She allowed herself to be patted on the head but refused to be
drawn up onto her lap.

"Do you have grandchildren?" Agatha asked. She knew that

Mrs. Bingham's daughter Beverly had a grown son, and she was vaguely aware of an older Bingham daughter.

"I do," said Mrs. Bingham.

Agatha felt triumphant for these were the first words the woman had ever addressed to her over coffee.

The little girl suddenly recognized Agatha and said she wanted to go to her apartment and watch cartoons.

"If your father and Lee Ann approve," Agatha told her, and she turned to ask Lee Ann, who had taken a chair on Agatha's side of the table but beyond Harriet.

Lee Ann nodded her approval and, to make conversation, asked, "How's Frederick?"

Agatha was glad to see a trace of shame in Lee Ann's eyes. "You know he had quite a shock," Agatha said in an accusatory tone, "but he's recovering. I've started a mental health support group for him."

Mrs. Bingham directed her fearsome scowl at Lee Ann and said, to Agatha's surprise, "Why don't you come to it?"

Lee Ann said, "Maybe I will. When does it meet?"

Agatha left the dining room with Jennie in hand, considering the irony of Lee Ann's attending the group while Frederick did not. She also wondered if Mrs. Bingham's scowl was unconscious and not meant to be frightening, because she had turned it on Lee Ann and then issued her a pleasant invitation.

On television she found *Sesame Street* and made Jennie a cup of cocoa. Then she sat at her kitchen table and wrote a note to Mrs. Bingham, enumerating her half-dozen mistakes of language. She placed the faulty English on the left and the preferred usage on the right. For example:

dang bit of difference	any difference
leastways	at least
you was visitin' Dad	you were visiting Dad

She underlined *visitin'* and wrote a sentence urging her to pronounce her final *g*'s instead of leaving them off words ending in *ing*.

When the Beezer men and Lee Ann came for Jennie, Agatha asked them about the scowl.

"Yep, it takes some getting used to all right," said Ernie.

His father explained that it was his sister's habit of trying to see the people she was talking to. "She's dang near totally blind, you know, and squintin' like that's the only way she can make out who it is."

When she was alone again, Agatha folded the note written in bold letters to Mrs. Bingham in half, carried it down the corridor and slipped it under the door of 120. Then she stepped across the hall to see Harriet, who invited her in for tea and a look at *Oprah*. She stayed for an hour, resisting all the while the urge to tell her about the crazy woman across the hall. She resisted because she was beginning to wonder whether the parole board might be correct, that Mrs. Bingham was not deranged after all, but simply a poor old woman out of her depth at Sunset Senior, and going blind besides.

Although the weatherman had predicted heavy snow and wind at some indefinite time in the future, maybe tonight, maybe tomorrow, Monday evening was balmy and still, and the crowd was three times the size of the week before.

John Beezer, with his sister, sat proudly in the front row as if he were responsible for the many people who came in and took seats at the dining tables. Janet Meers was among them. She hugged and kissed Agatha, and several women and a man followed her example. The man was Myron Kleinschmidt, a former congressman who many years earlier had thought of himself as Agatha's favorite sixth grader.

"Well, well, Miss McGee, it's wonderful to see you again, and looking so spry."

"You look fit yourself, Myron. Are you still living in Stagger-ford?"

"Yes, of course, where else? I live in the same house on Hemlock."

"I only ask because I haven't seen you in years."

"That's because you keep to yourself so much of the time, Miss McGee. I'm around and about every day." He gave the dining room a long admiring look. "You probably know that I was the one who got the federal money to build this place." Because Agatha was so short, he bent over to say confidentially, "The county commissioners said they were going to name it after me, but I guess they figured Sunset was better."

"It's not better, Myron, it's a terrible name for senior apartments. Sunset makes you think of the end of things, death and the like."

"Yes, I've often wondered who thought of it."

"The Kleinschmidt Apartments sounds just fine to me," she said, dismissing him in order to greet Bernice Dodson, who'd brought along two more of Agatha's former students.

But he persisted, saying, "Bless you, Miss McGee. I know of only one person in this town with enough clout to get the name changed."

"And who would that be?" she asked absently. She pictured Judge Caferty in her mind because Myron and the former judge were friends.

He said, "Why you, of course."

He continued to stand at her side, smiling benevolently upon the rest of the group as they entered and greeted Agatha. When they settled down and turned their attention to the front of the room, she began by saying, "We have a celebrity with us tonight," and introduced Congressman Kleinschmidt because she knew how badly he needed recognition.

There was vigorous applause as he stood up from his seat next to Mrs. Bingham and, facing the people, he clenched his hands over his head in a gesture of triumph. Then he said, "I give you Miss McGee." She knew he did this for a selfish reason—he wanted to see if applause for her would equal his. She guessed he must have been terribly disappointed, for hers was louder and longer lasting.

She thanked the group and said that they would each have a chance to introduce themselves after she made a few remarks about tonight's topic, lifelong friends.

Bernice interrupted her with a raised hand and a request that she announce the next week's topic beforehand so that the group had a chance to better prepare what they had to say. A number of others nodded their agreement, so Agatha said it was a good idea and off the top of her head she announced, "Next week let's talk about moral choices we have made during our lives and what sort of consequences they brought about."

While a few people rolled their eyes at each other—as if to say, This is truly the same old Miss McGee all right, her favorite subject has always been morality—the group showed its approval by applauding again. While they did so, she scanned the crowd. There was Mrs. Bingham squinting up at her from the front row. Behind her she recognized another six or eight former students and most of the other attendees. There were only four or five of the forty-odd people in the room she didn't know.

She spoke of the two lifelong friends she'd lost during the past Christmas season. She decided against describing their flaws of character along with their good points for what was the use of reminding the world of Thaddeus Druppers's obsessive fussiness or Lillian Kite's love of the *National Enquirer*? She went on and on about Lillian, much the dearer friend of these two old comrades, until tears sprang into her eyes and told her that she must stop. She was sure that no one in the room, except maybe Beverly and Janet, had ever seen her cry, and she didn't want to damage her reputation as a stoic.

When she opened the meeting to the stories of the participants, both Bernice Dodson and Myron Kleinschmidt stood up to speak at once. Agatha expected that Bernice, out of respect for age, would give up and sit down, or that Myron, out of respect for women, might do the same. But each of them, giving the other a withering look and expecting the other to relent, continued talking louder and louder. Finally, Agatha told them both to sit down and wait until all the others had finished.

She listened to about fifteen descriptions of old friends, and she was surprised to find herself referred to, by Beverly Bingham Mulholland, Harriet and Janet, as their dearest friend. Her heart swelled with pride for even John Beezer spoke up and said, "You bet, this Missus McGee is a real winner."

Myron, whom she called on last, spoke of his friendship with Judge Caferty, but then went on to praise Agatha, repeating what he'd told her earlier, that she was the only person he knew with enough clout to change the name of this building to the Kleinschmidt Senior Apartments.

When the meeting ended, Agatha was inundated by people from her past. They were a dizzyingly diverse group—two farmers, a young bureaucrat from the governor's staff, a biologist spending most of her adult life researching black bears and caterpillars, a flagman for the county highway department, a retired railroad engineer.

She returned to her apartment exhausted and with her head aswirl with everything she'd been told. Dropping into bed, she replayed the evening in her mind, and realized that she'd been applauded four times. This renewed her confidence to the point where she determined, falling asleep, to write to the county commissioners to propose a renaming of the Sunset Senior Apartments.

*   *   *

It would be only two or three weeks later when more people would show up than there were chairs to accommodate them and Myron Kleinschmidt would volunteer to ask the superintendent of schools if they could meet in the high school gymnasium.

29

The next morning Agatha went to work on her lesson plans. Even she was surprised by her eagerness to take up the subject of morality. She remembered feeling this way each year as she was about to start up the annual confirmation class at St. Isidore's, which she taught evenings over and above her sixth grade duties. After she'd listed half a dozen innocuous moral choices she'd made in her life, she put on her light raincoat and walked to the parish house, where she invited Father Healy to the next meeting.

"The topic is right up your alley, Father," she said while being ushered through the front of the mansion to his office at the back. "We're taking up morality."

He consulted a calendar on his desk and said, "I have a couple coming in for marriage preparation at seven, so I may be a few minutes late, but I'll be there. Thanks for the invitation."

"It's not my business, Father, but there is a strong aroma of bacon coming from your kitchen, and I've been told that bacon is the very worst thing for our cholesterol."

He laughed heartily and said, "Dr. Hammond tells me I have a strong heart, Miss McGee, so I'm assuming that it will withstand two strips of bacon each morning. By the way, how are you coming with your nemesis, the woman from prison?"

"I may be gaining the upper hand. It's too soon to tell, of course, but her behavior seems to be improving."

"Ah, and your hatred of her?"

Agatha searched her heart for hatred and found not a trace of it remaining. She shrugged and said, "I must be cured."

Her surprise must have shown on her face, because the priest said, "I can see you haven't had much more experience with hatred than I have. Otherwise you wouldn't look so amazed."

She said, "The woman still causes a strong reaction in me, Father, but it doesn't feel like hatred. It feels more like pity."

Father Healy clapped his hands. "That's exactly how it's supposed to work, Miss McGee. I don't mind admitting to you that of all the quotes of Jesus in the New Testament, I've had the hardest time with 'Love your enemies.' Yes, of course, I've proclaimed it from the pulpit but I never really knew how it worked until you conducted this experiment for me. Thank you, thank you for doing so, Miss McGee."

"It's not over yet, Father," she said, standing up to leave. "And it's a lot of hard work, but I guess I can say I'm happy to have done it for you. And for myself."

Passing through the foyer, she asked whether she could do him any more favors. "Any other experiments?" she said.

"No, but thank you very kindly," he answered, not understanding her facetiousness and then added, "But you can come and see me more often."

Why, this man really is fond of me, she thought as she allowed him to give her a brief hug at the door. She was shocked to hear herself say aloud, "I'm lucky to have lived so long." What she meant was that she was overcome with a degree of happiness such as she hadn't felt for many years. In a mere twelve weeks she'd moved out of her house, been present at a disinterment, taken part in a kidnapping and started a support group. Because of her Monday night meetings, she'd regained her identity in the community. Because of her progress with Mrs. Bingham— granted, it was grudging progress, but progress all the same—

she felt she hadn't entirely lost her teaching ability. For a moment she felt something close to ecstasy. In other words, she felt like a new woman.

Father Healy was looking at her intently, waiting for her to explain why she felt lucky to have lived so long, but Agatha, ever wary of sentimentality, said, "You really eat bacon every day, do you?"

"Only two pieces," he said, "and now with Lent coming on, I won't be having any until Easter."

Buttoning her coat and stepping out the door, she said, "Mend your ways, Father. Fourteen strips of bacon per week is dreadfully bad for your health."

30

TEN MONTHS LATER

Because it was quarter to seven on a Monday evening, Frederick Lopat locked up the big house on River Street and drove to the Kleinschmidt Apartments to pick up Agatha McGee and take her to the high school gymnasium. Winter was coming on—it was December third—and the car had barely warmed up before he parked in the space reserved for them in front of the school. He helped Agatha along the sidewalk and up to the front door, where his friend Albert Goltz, a former school janitor who had driven in from his house a couple of miles north of Willoughby, was waiting to hold open the door for them and to guide them along the dimly lit hallways, past the open door of the brightly lit gymnasium, to the stage door. Here Agatha insisted, as usual, that they leave her because she needed time to gather her thoughts.

Frederick and Albert returned along the corridor to the open door and entered the gymnasium. They took seats in the last row of three hundred folding chairs set up on the floor of the basketball court. Frederick, waiting for the meeting to begin, looked over the crowd. He saw Mayor Mulholland and his wife, Beverly, sitting in the front row next to Beverly's uncle, John Beezer. Tonight, for a change, John's son, Ernie Beezer; Ernie's daughter, Jennie; and his new wife, Lee Ann, had joined them. John Beezer's sister used to accompany him to every meeting, but she'd had a heart attack the past summer and died.

Next, and last, to arrive as a contingent from the Klein-schmidt Apartments were four or five women and a youngish man—that is, younger than Frederick, who was sixty-three— who shuffled and used a cane. Frederick counted 201 people, an average turnout. At the first meeting, nearly a year earlier, Agatha had told him, there had been just three people in attendance. Since moving the site to the high school, the lowest turnout had been last week when the first snow of the season and the impending Thanksgiving holiday had kept all but 84 people at home. There were certain weeks last summer, when many of Agatha's former students were back in town for high school reunions, that attendance had soared to nearly 400. In a contest of wills, Frederick had refused to attend until the gatherings outgrew the dining room of the Kleinschmidt Apartments. They had grown so large that he was no longer in danger of being called upon to speak.

As far as anyone knew, Staggerford was the only town in the United States to hold weekly meetings open to one and all. They weren't town meetings as such. There was nothing constitutional or official about them, and although politics came up as a topic often enough, no political party or candidate for office was ever endorsed. The meetings had been started by Agatha McGee as a support group for Frederick, who was down in the dumps over his lost girlfriend.

A round of vigorous applause greeted Agatha as she walked out onto the bare stage and took her place before the microphone. For a woman of eighty-eight, her stride and actions were sure and steady. Tonight's topic was changing careers, and she began by saying that she would dispense with her opening remarks on this subject because it was so foreign to her. "I was satisfied with my vocation as a sixth grade teacher for forty-odd years," she said. This elicited more applause from the group, which included at least two dozen of her former students.

"All right, who will begin?" she said and, as everyone expected, Myron Kleinschmidt stood up and spoke at length about how invigorating it had been to be elected to Congress at the age of forty-nine and, putting the best face on defeat, how inspiring it had also been to return to his law practice in Staggerford when his second term was over.

Albert Goltz whispered, "Bullshit," to Frederick, who nodded and smiled, as did two younger men in the row ahead of them. Albert's irreverence was one of the qualities Frederick was especially fond of.

Next to stand and speak was Bernice Dodson, who said she had seen this topic discussed on public television by Bill Moyers and some elderly guy who spoke of changing careers as "following your bliss." "It's a whole series of programs," she said, "and I recommend that everybody watch it because it's so fascinating."

There followed an argument about public TV, which Mrs. Severson called a channel for Democrats, saying that her late husband Wendell had forbidden her to watch it.

Someone asked her what was Democratic about it and she explained that it was supported at least partially by government funding. "Wendell was dead set against anything that the government paid for. Why, whenever we took a trip out west, we never visited the national parks because taxpayers' money went into them."

"Careful," Frederick said to Albert Goltz, but his friend could not contain himself. He told Mrs. Severson, "You very likely drove out west on roads paid for by the federal government." His voice booming, he declared to the audience at large, "Wendell Severson was the stupidest man I ever knew."

Mrs. Severson emitted a painful squeal. Frederick cringed. Agatha shook her finger at him, saying, "We aren't here to cast aspersions at one another, Mr. Goltz. If you can't exert more self-control than that, we'll have to ask you to leave."

Several people turned and glared at Goltz, as Frederick knew they would. The Monday night crowd always took Agatha's side in everything.

"No aspersion intended," Albert mumbled under his breath. "I'm only saying what's true."

A first-time member of the group diffused this little spat by standing up and saying, "I always wanted to go into singing, but I couldn't risk it financially." Frederick recognized him as the man who drove a Frito-Lay truck and distributed chips to bars, restaurants and grocery stores. Frederick remembered him singing "O Solo Mio" one day as he replenished the potato chip rack in Kruger's Pool Hall.

Agatha said he ought to try it anyhow. She said she'd read an article that said people who changed careers and went into something they loved usually proved successful at it.

"But I've got a wife and two kids to support," explained the potato chip man.

"It makes no difference," she continued. "The same article said that anybody who took this risk, particularly in an artistic field such as singing, came out ahead financially as well as professionally."

Facing a sea of doubtful expressions she added, "Well, it stands to reason, doesn't it? Going into a field you love, you'll throw yourself into it wholeheartedly. You'll work so hard that your income will accrue to you without your realizing it. Henry David Thoreau said something interesting on this subject. He said, 'If you have built castles in the air . . . ; that is where they should be. Now put the foundations under them.' "

The potato chip man got up and left. Frederick wondered if her words had disgusted him or if he wanted to start singing full time immediately.

Then a number of people stood up and described career

changes in lives they knew about, some of which were successful, others not—from banking to oil painting, from operating
dog kennels to becoming a grocer, from digging ditches to
cemetery maintenance. All of it struck Frederick as pretty boring. But then he was suddenly brought out of a daydream by
Agatha's saying, "Frederick can tell us about a career change of
his own that worked out just fine." He immediately scrambled
to his feet and broke into a sweat while she explained further,
"It was nearly ten years ago that he became Willoughby's rural
mail carrier, so he was in his early fifties at the time. Frederick?"

"I used to be the Indian out at the tourist center," he
mumbled, "but then I got this civil service job in Willoughby . . .
and . . . I guess that's about it."

He sat down quickly but was forced to his feet again by several people who asked him questions, which he answered shyly:

"Nope, I haven't got a drop of Indian blood in me."

"I guess I got the job because I looked like an Ojibway."

"Yeah, it got kinda dicey toward the end. A bunch of people
from the reservation thought the job should go to a real Indian.
Another bunch thought the job ought to be done away with."

"Sure, we're related. Agatha's my great-aunt. See, my
grandpa was her brother."

The meeting lasted slightly over an hour and a half. The last
item of business was to assign next week's topic. Bernice Dodson wondered if they could take up a subject they'd handled before, namely, lifelong friends, and Agatha approved. She said
this was a topic she'd had experience with and they could expect her to speak for up to ten minutes at the start of the meeting the next Monday. Several people waited while Frederick and
Albert Goltz helped her down the steps from the stage, then
surrounded her, the few strangers introducing themselves and
the others inquiring about her health.

Her answer was always the same, "I can't complain for my
age." Tonight she added, "Lately I've been thinking there's

something obscene about a woman of eighty-eight being as fit as I am."

Frederick knew she was proud of the state of her health. She'd told him more than once that except when she'd been in for a pacemaker, her last hospitalization had been at the time of her birth. But standing at her side, Frederick kept one of his large hands on her back, between her shoulders, because he also knew how tired she was. These Monday night meetings exhausted her.

She admitted as much on the way home. Half to herself—but Frederick heard it—she said, "I'm much too old to be carrying on like this week after week." Louder she said, "I've been thinking of giving up this job, Frederick." He knew she was bluffing. It was these weekly meetings that fueled her engine, as Albert Goltz would have said. They energized her, kept her going. He recalled her diminished state the previous winter, when she still lived in the big house on River Street and the water pipes in the basement had frozen and burst. When he finally got home from work after a blizzard had trapped him for nearly twenty-four hours, he thought he was looking death in the face.

Pulling up in front of the Kleinschmidt Apartments, he decided to call her bluff. "I'll come for you again next Monday?" he asked.

"Of course, Frederick." She opened her door, then quickly shut it against the cold wind. "Why wouldn't you?"

"Well, you said you were thinking of giving up the meetings."

With a sly smile she said she'd been joking. "There's no possibility I'd give them up, Frederick. I get far too much out of them ever to give them up. Besides, they're better than sleeping pills. They wear me out so that I get a good night's sleep. I'll go in now and I'll sleep like a baby."

But she didn't go in. Warming to her subject, she remained in the car, saying, "Several years ago when I had bursitis in my shoulder, I went to physical therapy."

Frederick remembered very clearly. He'd had to drive her to Mercy Hospital three times a week for a month or more.

" 'Range of motion,' the therapist kept saying. 'You must not lose your range of motion.' She meant if I gave up certain movements of my arm I might not ever get them back. So she had me raising my arm and lowering it, working around the pain to make sure I could still do it. Well, I believe 'range of motion' applies to our psyches as well as our bodies, Frederick. If we shut down parts of our thinking, we'll never get them back, and so you might say these Monday nights are my psychological therapy."

She paused for a moment, then said, "Does that make any sense, Frederick?"

"Sure," he said. When had she ever made anything but sense?

"All right, thanks for the ride. Goodnight, Frederick."

He watched her hurry in through the wide front door and turn down the hallway to her apartment.